TITAN GAMES

MARK TOOHEY

A NOVEL

Titan Games

© Mark Toohey 2024

All rights reserved. No part of this publication may be reproduced, stored in a retrieval system, or transmitted in any form or by any means, electronic, mechanical, photocopying, recording or otherwise, without the prior written permission of the author.

ISBN: 978-1-7638682-0-5 (eBook)
ISBN: 978-1-7638682-1-2 (Paperback)

Printed in Australia

Editor: Marisa Parker

Published by Mark Toohey and Dry Rain Publishing

I would like to thank the Situk River for feeding me, and the Tlingits of Yakutat for including me onto their lands to watch my children grow.

CHAPTER 1

Though the war on drugs, etc., had ended (drugs won, by the way), Guantanamo Bay remained a legal black hole.

SHE LOVES HER office. Though it is small, and any view of the city across Pitt Street is blocked by a newer, taller building, it is private and has her name on the door—Helen Ellis. It is an office she has earned. Marketing and Promotional Diplomas from thirty years ago hang on the wall alongside awards she has won over her career, but the awards themselves are old now. Heading up advertising campaigns has become few and far between.

Once she was the 'Go to Girl', for fresh ideas. But somehow over the years, she has become the 'Go get girl': "Go get Helen to help"; "Go get Helen to check the numbers"; "Go get Helen to organise that". Then she was suddenly middle-aged. She doesn't know what happened in between. But it has enabled her, as a single woman, to buy a small house close to the city where she has always wanted to live. She appreciates that, though the payments are tough.

Slipping behind her desk with her morning latte, five minutes early as always, Phillip from Accounts leans in through her door.

"He wants to see you."

Helen leaves her latte on the desk and headed down the hall to the boss's office. He is not yet forty and has taken over after a merger with another company. Helen thinks he has an air of entitlement about him, though it is not something she would say out loud.

He leans back against his desk, waiting for her. "Hand Financial Services?"

"Yes." She waits for more information, but he is not forthcoming. "Ah, a five-million-dollar contract. I promoted them as 'Safe

Hands'. But that was months ago."

"They are bankrupt. They filed yesterday."

Helen slumps into a chair. Her shoulder-length brown hair flops forward as she cups her face in her hands. "I feel sick. A thousand people will lose their homes."

"And it's a better look if OUR company is the one seen to be acting responsibly," he says.

"Yes. Of course."

"So, pack up your desk, Helen. We have to let you go."

"What?" Her big, brown eyes look up from the carpet, her brow furrowed. "Let me?"

*

Five scrambling months have passed, and Helen finds herself alone in a windowless office. It began with a string of job interviews, but they all turned out the same. She was always: "too experienced for the position" or, "it would be too big a step down for you" or, her diplomas were simply "too old." It was even more disheartening to be informed, "You're not in the right age bracket for THIS particular product."

And the questions they asked were just as depressing: "Have you thought about retraining?" As well intentioned as their suggestions were, it didn't help.

The last straw was being asked: "Where do you see yourself in twenty years?" She doesn't want to think about that. Not at fifty-three years!

It was time she backed herself, Helen had then decided. This led to a bank loan and the refinancing of her home to start her own business. But now, after months of expensive advertising, she has only received two small contracts. And they are basic works that last only a couple of weeks, promoting new local family business openings. They didn't pay much. No one has been through the door to see her diplomas on the wall, and she is beginning to think she lives with, and on, a laptop. Things are tight. She isn't broke yet, but she is well and truly on the way.

Helen sits, picking at a thread on her woollen jumper like an old love wound; she knows she shouldn't, but cannot stop. She knows better than to wind it around her finger and tug too hard in case it all unravels, but she cannot put it back either or leave it alone. It is somehow comforting to have it there. Far more comforting than the bright red notice stamped across the envelope from the bank, that is lying on her desk.

"Oh God," she sighs, claustrophobia taking over as she tears it open. It reads bad news, and her heart starts to race. She drops the notice on the desk and begins picking at the thread, again.

I need air, she decides. Getting up, she makes her way out the door of her home office and walks down her narrow driveway, kicking off her shoes as she goes.

For some reason, the air feels thinner. She puts her hands on her hips and sucks harder. It isn't enough and her hands drop to her knees in an ugly squat, as she heaves for more oxygen, as if she has just completed her first marathon.

"Oh, God!" Huff. "Oh, dear!" Puff. "Oh, shit …"

After a minute or two, Helen straightens up and composed herself, somewhat, and heads for the door to her house.

Entering her quaint, inner city, two-bedroom home, she makes a beeline for the fridge. Pouring herself a half glass of wine, she chugs the lot. She rubs her forehead deeply. Taking her glass in one hand and the bottle in the other, she departs back to her renovated garage office. She pauses at her shoes along the way, and 'Professional Helen' almost takes back control. But on careful consideration, day drinking in a driveway seems appropriate about now. She leaves them there, pours another drink, and strolls off.

Helen leaves the door open and puts the bottle on the desk where it will be handy.

"Brrrr," she whispers, blowing a raspberry at the ceiling.

Then, glass in hand, she checks her phone out of habit. It has become a nasty habit that has developed through hope and worry, and over the ever-increasing amount of time she has on her hands, sitting in an empty office.

This time though, a message blinks back at her. She puts it on speaker.

"Hello, I am Janine Buckman from the Wongii Development Fund, and we need promotional work as soon as possible. We are a community, not a business, but money has been set aside from fundraising. Please return my call."

"Fundraising?"

She types 'Wongy' Development on her laptop and it suggests the spelling to Wongii. *Never heard of it,* she thinks. But the headlines and bylines are interesting.

Gas Running Dry. Town rejects coal for organics.

Lights out for Wongii? Remaining 60 workers have 60 days.

Ambitious Solar Plan Seeks Investors.

Helen looks down at the bank statement lying there like a newly discovered sinkhole, wondering how deep and dark it will get, and then looks back to her screen. She takes another swig of wine and places her glass on the statement. Putting her head down, she starts researching all facets of Wongii.

*

Four young men walk past cow droppings in a paddock. Two carried javelins, one a sack, and they all sport a bike helmet.

As they step onto the red carpet and pass the golf pin, Aaron Buckman, a tall, twenty-one-year-old athlete with blond shaggy hair, stops. He reaches into the sack and drops two circular discuses onto the carpet. "You're blue. You're pink," he announces, lying the sack down.

Chris and Ben each pick up their discus. Chris is twenty-six, of medium height and of a solid build. He begins stretching his arms over his head, leaning from side to side. "I got to warn you, I've been getting some practice in."

"Oh, did you hear that, Aaron? Chris has been practising," states Billy Uke, standing back from the others with his javelin. His big smile flashes beneath a mop of dark curls. A tall, Koori Aboriginal, and in the best shape a twenty-one-year-old can be in, Billy came second in the State Decathlon Championship, a year and a half earlier. He surprised most people, but it was no surprise to Aaron. Best friends since they could remember, it is Aaron's grandfather, Jack, who trains Billy. And Aaron has always tagged along in training. He is nearly as good as Billy, but not quite.

"That's not going to help you," Aaron comments to Billy. *Cocky, always cocky.*

"Or him!" Ben says, stretching his calf muscles. "It's all about speed, man." Ben is lanky, ginger-haired, and a complete stoner.

"No. It's power and accuracy, my friend. Power and accuracy," retorts Chris.

There are two more golf pins, set out as a three-holed game, each 200-metres apart. The course is hilly and on uneven ground, making it easy to trip or step into a divot. This is a race, not a golf tournament. It does not matter how many times you throw the disc, though it does help to throw straight, and the disc has to stay on the carpet for completion of the hole.

Billy and Aaron are to start with a handicap to keep the race fair.

The handicap is set with the javelins. After a few minutes more of stretching for everybody, they are ready to begin.

With javelins in hand, Aaron and Billy eye each other off and take three steps back— the preset distance. They rock back and forth twice, taking the javelin as far back as their arms allowed. On the third rock, they run in, side by side, and launch them from the carpet. Both are good throws, but Billy's sails past Aaron's. He turns to Aaron, grins and wiggles his eyebrows; Aaron always hates that.

"That's what I like to see," Chris claps. "A fair chance."

They start strapping on their bike helmets and pulling them tight. This is a learned lesson from the regular Friday event, after a guy named Pete finished with a concussion on the second hole. That hole proved itself too far from the road and medical attention, and Pete didn't want to play anymore. Helmets on, Billy and Aaron walk down to their respective javelins as a starting point. Ben and Chris stay on the red carpet as their starting point and practise their discus spin.

*

Wongii is a small town, set in a long valley, on the Southern Tablelands, population of 800. The original buildings are from the 1940s, but most of the town centre has been built in the early 70s when the power company arrived. The buildings appear run down and 'daggy', now.

The valley itself has always been quite beautiful, with deep green fields of prime dairy fields that have arisen after settlement. But it has never been more colourful than when the Dairy Corporations screwed the price of milk down so low that it sent the dairy farmers broke.

Since then, smaller, brighter fields of organic permaculture have sprung up in their place. These are separated by goat paddocks, free-range chickens, and buses. Lots of buses …

The buses are painted in crazy designs and loud colours. Entire families of hippies live in them. There are the New Age Hippies, the Grunge type, and, of course, the old Flower Power Hippies.

In the town centre, there were even 'hipsters' fighting a losing battle in their attempt to gentrify the place and give it some class.

The only blemishes are the ugly gas wells dotted throughout the landscape, and a large overhead power line running the length of the valley from the power station.

There is only one bar situated in the Wongii Hotel. The hotel car park is out the back of the building, facing up the hill from where Billy and Aaron have thrown their javelins. Twenty men are drinking and gambling on the event, like they do every Friday afternoon.

"The handicap is set gentlemen," a farmer calls.

Billy's coach, Jack Buckman, holds up his money straight away. Jack is an imposing man for seventy years of age; large and tough, still working every day on the farm after fifty-five years. He has a thick white beard and a smile that is not to be trusted. Jack is known to be mischievous and jolly throughout the area, but as any of the old timers will tell you, he can turn cantankerous when his patience runs out. "I'll take $20 on Billy."

"I don't know, Jack. That's a big start for Ben. He may be a stoner, but he can run." Declares Mr Exley, a farmer.

"And Aaron almost beat him last time," Mike, the power-worker, in his high-vis shirt, steps in and takes the bet. "Only ten metres in it." Jack doesn't reply. Instead, he holds up another $20 note to Mike. "Ok, you're on," he takes that bet too.

"My, someone is confident this week. Been giving a bit of extra training, or did you slip something into one of the kid's drinks?" Asks Dale.

Dale is Jack's friend since childhood, yet looks ten years younger. Another farmer, Dale, is fit, clean shaven, gay, and with a dignity that seems to balance out Jack's gruffness. He is also accompanied by a goat on a leash. It willingly follows him around like a dog. He does this mainly to upset Jack.

There is something very wrong about Rubi the goat. No breeder wants her anywhere near their flock. She is spectacularly ugly: her tail points left, one horn is curled, while the other is straight and points right, and one of her eyes is wonky, forever looking up. But Dale loves her, and she clings to Dale like a toddler.

"You're the only one who needs something slipped into his drink, old man. And keep that freak away. No dogs allowed in the beer garden!" Grumbles Jack.

"Oh, stop it. She is adorable. We can't all be a 'Sir Linneus', you know."

"My Sir Linneus is a pedigree, with the finest cashmere in the valley. No one's sure that's a goat," Jack points out.

"Come Rubi, there is money to be made," he turns his back to Jack and calls, "Fifty on Billy, please, gentlemen."

*

Billy stands behind his javelin, looking up the hill to Chris and Ben, who are waiting with their discus in hand. He is confident that he has Chris covered. Ben is fast enough, but over three holes, chance comes into play, and one miss-throw can add thirty metres to a hole. Aaron is his concern. Always his concern. He knows he has a slight edge over him, but it really is slight. And if Aaron had not experimented with weed and alcohol that spring, he would have faced him in the State Decathlon Championships as well. Today, all of that has passed and Aaron is back to his best.

Billy places his hand on the javelin and begins his usual rocking. When he pulls it free, the race will begin. He sees Aaron sink lower in his stance. He rocks again, and Chris and Ben wind their arms back. He pulls the javelin free and takes off. Aaron bolts into a sprint at the same time. Ben and Chris spin forward and hurl their discs.

The sound of twenty gamblers cheering in unison rolls up the hill to reach them, and Rubi faints. The fact that Rubi is a fainting goat is the most annoying part to Jack. She falls and rolls, legs up, but no one even notices.

Billy is almost there. Aaron reaches into the sack and takes his disc out. He spins around and lets the disc fly, rushing off the carpet to give chase. Billy steps on, moments later, and drops his javelin. He reaches into the sack and grabs … a snake. Its tail flicks his upper forearm, and he lets out a cry, "Arghh!"

He jumps back, drops the sack, stumbles, and falls over. He shoots a filthy look at Aaron. "You rotten bastard," he mumbles.

Aaron looks back, laughing. Billy springs to his feet, runs around the sack to grab the bottom and upends it. A diamond python slithers away. He grabs his disc, but the damage is already done; Aaron has pulled further ahead and has a greater lead than when the race began. Billy goes into his spin and makes sure it travels straight.

Aaron's next throw is straight and true and strikes Chris on the thigh, bringing him crashing down. Chris is still on all fours rubbing his leg when Aaron collects the discus lying beside him. "Fore."

"Bit late arsehole," Chris yells after him.

Billy is still last at the first golf pin, but his disc is close and it only needs scooping up and tossing onto the carpet. He retrieves it and begins again. He is starting to recover ground and Chris isn't far off.

"Fore," he screams ahead to Chris for no reason other than to take advantage of him being struck earlier. Chris drops to the ground and covers up. Billy dashes past him, giving a cheeky grin.

Aaron is closing in on Ben at the second hole, and Billy is still one discus throw behind them. He has no chance and can only hope one of their throws goes wide. He sprints hard between deliveries, his throws sail dead straight. He does everything right, but it is not enough.

Aaron takes the lead at the final hole. Ben throws slightly to the left and Billy gives it all he has to gain from it, but try as he might, Ben just holds out for second place. Aaron wins, with Billy third, and Chris limps in with no sympathies whatsoever.

*

Drinking and good humour fill the betting ring as the bets are settled, and the contestants make their way across the paddock to the carpark.

Jack has a beer in one hand and a hot sausage sandwich in the other. He tries being philosophical about the outcome. "Ah, well. That's what I get for training a vegan!"

"Christ, Jack, how many times do we have to explain?" Tom, a grunge-style hippie in ragged jeans, reminds him. "He's not even vegetarian, he just doesn't do chemicals. *I'm the vegan*! Well … I'm a vegan who has relapses with bacon. Man, bacon is as hard as nicotine to give up."

A clean cut, thirty-year-old hipster with a hat starts nodding. "Uh, huh, I'm a vegetarian, but still bust out for a seafood platter at Christmas. Prawns!"

Jack outstretches his arms. "Why is my fridge full of hummus when hippies have bacon and prawns?" They are all hippies to Jack.

"Because your daughter says meat is killing the planet, and your doctor says it's killing you," Dale snatches the sausage sandwich from his hand and bins it.

The contestants arrive and Aaron is congratulated. Punters pat him on the back, and he is happy to accept the win, but he can't resist looking back to make sure Billy is watching. He is. The crowd disperses for the pub, and Chris for an icepack to stop the swelling, leaving Aaron, Billy, and Jack.

"Well done," Jack says. "And a good hard run, Billy."

"Thanks, Grandpa. I gave it my best today," Aaron says with a smirk.

"He put a snake in the sack."

Jack chuckles. "Did he, now? Well, it doesn't take anything away from your efforts, does it?"

Mike the power-worker returns. "Here's the $50 from Dale. And here is your forty bucks back. Thanks for the heads-up, Jack."

"You bet against me?" Asks Billy. "You are my coach! Is that even legal?"

"Where do you think he got the snake from?" Jack snickers and pockets the money. He pulls his car keys out and gives them to Aaron. "Make sure you both get to the meeting tonight. Why the town is wasting money on an outsider, when your mother could do it all herself, I don't know. She never listens to me, anyway. But you both better get along."

"What about you?" Aaron asks.

"Well, I have to buy Dale a drink now, don't I?" He walked off.

The boys stand there watching his back as he re-enters the pub. "Did he set me up to lose, just so he could cheat Uncle Dale out of fifty lousy bucks?" Mutters Billy.

"Ah, yeah he did," Aaron exhales with a twinkle of admiration.

*

The Buckman house is a large wooden home with verandas all round, built in the late 1940s. It has been well maintained and painted over the generations and sits on eighty acres with a barn, a sprawling vegetable garden, and a perfect, professional, single lane training track with a sandbox at the end.

The home consists of four generous bedrooms and a large living room with wide double doors leading out to the veranda. But it is the large kitchen and big kitchen table that are the centre of the home. It is always cluttered, always busy, clean, yet lived in.

Janine Buckman leans across the table stacking folders; her long blonde hair is dishevelled and hanging across it as well. Her graceful and calm manner is in stark contrast to her father, though at times he can test this, but it has enabled her to move effortlessly between farmer, worker, and hippie. She has worked tirelessly for her town in trying to avoid the coming storm of unemployment and climate change.

Bundling the folders under her arm, she is about to leave when Aaron comes through the backdoor and heads straight to the refrigerator. "Hi, Sweetie. It's a left-over night, I'm afraid." She sees Aaron put Jack's truck keys on the fridge top. "Where's your grandfather?"

"At the pub."

"Working on his Feng Shui again, is he? Do you want me to wait?"

"No. Billy is going to pick me up. I'll see you there," Aaron replies.

CHAPTER 2

HELEN TAKES PRIDE in being diligent and has studied everything about Wongii. She knows the history, the financial distress, and has a comprehensive knowledge of the power company, Lassiter's Resources, along with the distribution of their overhead power lines.

Helen has spent hours on the phone with Janine and has double checked her own figures. She understands how imperative it is for the town and the importance of the town meeting. She also knows she needs this to work for her; she does not want to think of the consequences, if it doesn't.

Helen is confident she is prepared and ready. The thing she is not prepared for is the sound of beating drums and the smell of dope wafting through her car as she swings into the Wongii Town Hall car park.

She passes a work truck with four power workers in high-vis shirts standing around it drinking beer. On the other side of the car park, fire twirls brilliantly in the hue of the setting sun. Helen pulls into a vacant spot and flicks off the engine. Four people in a circle bang away on tom toms, as two fire twirlers put on a show.

"Oh, great!" She huffs. *Why hadn't Janine warned me about this?*

Helen defines two distinct groups: a pseudo tribe of thirty-five or so 'Alternative People' and hippies smoking weed and dancing to tom toms to her left; and to the right, the 'Soon to be Unemployed' power-worker, and 'Old Time Farmers' cooling off with a beer after work. Between them, looking amused by it all, are a few Koori families sitting on the town hall steps. Each group's children are playing together, screaming and running about wildly, in a mass game of chasing— up and down the steps, around the work trucks, and through the dancing hippies.

*

Caramelised onion on the side, Jack butters his white bread as two fat sausages bubble away in a pan of grease. With the television on, and with another beer waiting, he is happy to be alone tonight and is going to take full advantage. There is no Janine to stop him, there is time to clean up and hide the evidence, and he has fifty dollars in his pocket from Dale to boot.

Jack admires his culinary skills before taking a bite and savouring the taste. "Oh, dear lord, that's good." He grabs his plate and leaves the kitchen to eat on the veranda, where a beer awaits him. On the way, a name that is mentioned on the television catches his ear and stops him in his tracks.

"I don't quite know what to say after that, Sandra," admits Stan, the news presenter. "Other than that, Toby Costello will be taking a holiday of some fashion, in the not too distant future."

"Very sad. Horrible for the victim, I know," says Sandra, the co-host. "But I can't help but feel sorry for Toby, as well. Coming up after the break: breadboards and bathmats! Are they ever really clean?"

"I know Toby," Jack reaches for the remote control.

*

The town hall sits at the centre of Wongii and is in need of some repair and paint work. Built in 1964, the weathered weatherboard exterior houses tall windows, much like an old church. It is all wood, from the outside to the interior wall panels and exposed wooden rafters, to the wide wooden floorboards that sounds like a freight train when a chair is dragged across them.

Helen stands before the onlookers, on a stage that is only two steps above floor level, with Janine sitting at a table covered with folders alongside her.

"Ahh, but we tried a Co-Op. It failed miserably and half the town left. We've got more dreadlocks than jersey cows now," sixty-four-year-old Mr Exley points out to Helen. He is stocky, bald, and usually abrupt.

"That was a Dairy Co-Op," Helen reminds the room. "Fifteen years ago, you had a dairy industry and a gas industry. Now … you have neither."

"We do have coal. And if these clowns decided to use it, we wouldn't be having this meeting," a power worker calls out.

Organic farmers, alternative people, hippies and Kooris alike, object loudly to being called clowns. Helen waves at them to be quiet. "You cannot promote a combination of organic food AND coal. You will never find an investor. However—"

"Investors like Lassiter's Resources?" An old, grey-haired Koori man asks. "Take the money and nick off?"

"I've seen this show before," an even older farmer declares. "Investment 'trickle-down economics' washed my livelihood away. I preferred standing in cow shit."

"I am trying to help. You cannot do this alone," Helen knows she needed to wrest back control of the room. "You people, between you all right here," she nods, "can combine organic meals and produce, with carbon neutral accommodation, to help find that investor. It is just marketing. Something like … 'Wongii Healthy Living. Stay the weekend and put a week on your life!'" Helen sweeps her hand across the air like reading a billboard.

"No one wants to stay in a town where buses don't have wheels,"

Mr Exley motions towards a woman of thirty-five with piercings. Her bright pink hair is shaved on one side.

"No one wants to hear from a man reminiscing about his cow," she waves him away, and people snigger.

"But it is a start." *Common ground, bring them back to common ground.* "I suggest a logo to clarify local values and link everyone. Clean energy and organics, or chemical-free and fossil fuel-free … whatever common ground you can find. As long as you can cross-promote one another. We can then build a functioning peer network. Promote. Run competitions. Hold a festival."

"Festival of the absurd," a heckler calls. "Go home to your soy latte."

*

Sitting forward in the lounge, Jack watches the debacle for the second time. "Bloody idiot!"

After a mild bumper accident in the rain, the clip on the television shows the driver of the car behind alighting from his vehicle apologising, but Toby begins pushing at him. Jack does not remember Toby Costello being so built up with muscle when, eighteen months ago, he beat Billy in the State Championship. He has gone on to take the Australian title.

A news presenter is speaking over the top of the clip: "Here we have Australian Decathlon Champion Toby Costello going from Olympian, to Titan, to prison."

When the driver retreats around the car to get away, Toby tears off his windshield wiper and gives chase. Round and round the car, Toby whips him. The man has no hope of getting away. Police arrive and are forced to tackle Toby to the ground.

"Fool, you should know better." Jack shakes his head and turns off the television. "Titans. Pfff." He chuckles and heads for his beer on the veranda.

Something begins to gnaw at him, though, and his mind ticks over in the solitude of the evening. He isn't halfway through his sausage sandwich when his brow furrows and his blood pressure rises. He rushes to his room and begins digging out old newspaper sports pages and official track results he has kept. He ruffles through them, running a finger down the pages, letting them fall to the floor if they are of no use. He doesn't read any articles; he only needs times and names. He stops; there it is! Jack dashes to the kitchen for his truck keys.

*

"The Wongii Development Fund will require a backup battery for the town. That is $200,000," Helen announces to the room as Jack slid his truck to a stop across the gravel car park.

The room gasps at the price, and some simply throw up their hands. Helen allows time for the figure to sink in. She notices the door swing open at the back of the room and a large, bearded man enters. "But if you can turn one light bulb on in another town, some of you will keep your jobs."

Jack makes his way up one side of the room, pushes forward between people, then retreats. "Only six weeks till I'm out of work," a power worker calls to her. Jack is near the front now, checking each row of chairs.

"But it becomes commercially viable …" she tries to ignore Jack, rubbing his hands together with a fool's grin, "… to attract investors," she continues.

The bearded man drags an empty chair out of his way, and it squeals its objection. He interrupts and calls from across the room, "There you are. Billy, I want to talk to you."

"Excuse me?" Helen keeps her tone polite. Jack is too focused to hear her. "Billy, my boy."

"Sir!" Helen's tone changes.

"*Dad!* What are you doing?" Janine jumps to her feet and Jack stops cold.

"Dad?" Helen looks at Janine.

"What's up, Grandad?" Aaron asks.

"Billy is off to the Games, that's what."

"No, Jack." Billy shakes his head, "I didn't enter the Olympic Trials. You have to do the Trials."

"Oh, not the Olympics. The Titan Games, Guantanamo Bay."

The words Guantanamo Bay set off mutterings amongst the farmers, but the alternatives and hippies erupt in protest with a loud chorus: "Noooo!"

"What the hell is he talking about?" A Koori Auntie asks.

"Our Billy?" Mr Exley asks.

"Oh, stop it, Dad. No one is going to Guantanamo Bay. Are you drunk?" Janine queries.

"No, I'm not drunk!" Jack pauses. "Well, I've had a couple. But I'm okay."

"Oh, God!" Janine puts a hand to her face.

Helen resignedly takes a step back. *This looks like it could descend into a family argument.* The meeting has already descended into unfamiliar grounds, and she knows better to stay out.

"Now hear me out, darling. I know how to get Billy into the Games run by the pharmaceutical companies!" Jack turns to Billy.

"Your points are still good from last year. Toby Costello—"

"The Titan Games are a disgrace," interrupts Billy.

"I know that," Jack replies, as if he has stated the obvious.

"Yeah, they are!" Yells an alternative woman, and the chorus begins again: "Rotten drug companies! Is he for real?" People rail against Jack.

Jack turns to face them. "How can YOU lot be so against drugs, for God's sake?" He points to a questionable looking fifty-year-old … fifty hard years. "You're not even nice without the acid!" He retorts.

"Listen, Toby—"

"Wait on. Isn't Guantanamo Bay a US Military Prison? But in Cuba?" The old Koori calls.

"Oh, it's not a prison anymore," the woman with the pink hair and shaved side explains. "The Titan Games make enough money for ten prisons."

"But is this the Druggos' Olympics we are talking about?" Mr Exley asks her.

"Yeah, dude. But they are Titan druggos, not Olympian," a twenty-three-year-old stoned hippie answers. With his bloodshot eyes glowing, he raises an arm in the air to Mr Exley: "Like in Greek Mythology—'Release the Kraken'!" He drops his hand with a dramatic command.

"Ahh, 'Release the Crack Head' is more like it," Mr Exley spits. "The Kraken was Nordic, you fool!"

"Roidrage! Roadrage!" He corrects. "He's locked up," Jack interrupts desperately.

"Tut tut, Jack. You are beginning to speak 'in tongues'," Dale teases.

The room sniggers at Jack, but he will not give up. Defiant, and a little drunk, he yells, "With or without drugs, my boy can hold his own against those cheating bastards."

"You're mad, you old bugger," his 'vegan, grunge hippie' friend says.

"Put your mung beans where your mouth is," Jack holds up a $20 note.

Janine raises a hand high to the room, and it surprises Helen how many fall quiet. "Enough," she calls, looking directly at her father. The entire room goes silent.

Jack seizes the opportunity and appeals directly to Helen one last time. "I say the Titan Games. Where advertising is welcomed. You want to promote Wongii? Put a t-shirt on this one," he places a hand on Billy's shoulder.

"I'm not going Jack," Billy insists.

Helen steps in alongside Janine. "Hold on. What do you mean by his points are still good?"

Billy opens his hands to Aaron, stating, "What? Am I invisible?"

Jack ignores him. "Titans work on a national ratings system. Toby Costello, Australia's best, just got arrested for being a 'roided up madman. And our second and third best are on the Olympic Squad. Billy's points are next in line. He already qualifies for Decathlon."

"You are that good?" Helen asks Billy.

Aaron jumps in before Billy can object again. "Yes. He absolutely is."

"Right or wrong, the Titan Games are a massive form of advertising," Helen announces to the room.

"You can't be serious?" Janine is flabbergasted.

"This is an opportunity to exhibit the results of a Wongii lifestyle. To showcase the town as a tourist spot, as an organic hub, as a *healthy* place," Helen's voice rings out. "All run on clean energy." She sounds upbeat and confident, and the locals start to respond, first with murmurs within the groups, and then between the groups. She gives them time.

"A clean athlete in the 'Olympics of Drug Enhancement' is a *fantastic* way to attract investors," she continues. "It is all about promotion. And *this* is something I can work with, I can exploit." The crowd is nodding agreement. "This will exploit itself!"

"Go Ukey," someone calls from the back. Other voices rise in agreement: "Oh wow!"

"Titan Billy!"

"Wongii Titan!" Applause sweeps through the room, and it is decided.

Billy is gobsmacked and glares at Jack and Aaron. Jack nods back with a winner's grin, and Aaron laughs at him.

*

The sun is popping up and Billy quietly makes his way along the veranda to the Buckman kitchen. Ready for his morning run, today, he has a bone to pick with Aaron.

How could he think I have any chance against the world's best, especially after they have been doped up? I can't compete against steroids. The same thoughts have been running in a loop since he woke up, and he is still lost in it when Janine mischievously jumps out of the doorway to startle him.

"Boo! Word is out about the Decathlon. Our webpage group has doubled because of you." She carries a basket and is chirpy and high-spirited. Aaron is right behind her.

"All the way to eighteen."

"It still counts. I'll have omelettes ready when you get back." She leaves for the chicken coup.

In the silence that follows, Aaron knows Billy is perturbed about the previous night's meeting. The two quietly face off.

"What are you doing to me?" Billy asks.

"What? You don't want an omelette?"

"Hey. Why are you two standing around doing nothing?" Jack yells from the vegetable garden. He is waving a pitchfork at them. "You think you're training for Parliament?"

"Why is there a frypan full of sausage grease in my kitchen?" Janine yells over her shoulder.

Jack puts his head down and returns to work.

CHAPTER 3

LONG TABLES HAVE been pushed together in the Town Hall and twenty people sit around brainstorming ideas.

It has been decided that a festival will be the 'kick off' and local musicians have formed a blues band. The gathering, of course, consists of the unavoidable mixed bag of people that Wongii has on offer, but Helen is surprised to see Mr Exley show up. She is chairing the meeting and has her laptop open, listening to Julian, a skinny, balding forty-four-year-old artist who she thinks looks like the singer, Sting.

"We have a lot of artists, and aspiring artists. We could hold a competition and exhibition. There are a lot of people on the South Coast, just like us."

"Problem is 'just like us' don't have any money either. Nah, get the families in. Every kid wins a prize," Mr Exley says.

"That's a good idea," Billy's mother, Mary, chimes in. Forty-four, and only 167 cm, Mary is where Billy got his mop of hair and ready smile from. "What about a giant ring toss with hula hoops then? ... Laddie could hammer together a deck to throw from. A prize under every fence post."

Her husband, Laddie, is much taller and still fit at forty-seven.

As Mary speaks, he mimes her words with an expressive face to a very sweet looking four-year-old hippy child. He brings two fingers together and encompasses a large circle and begins tossing his imaginary rings about the room. He follows this with pretending to hammer a nail but hits his thumb. She is giggling along at his antics.

"Oh, you like that idea, do you? And what's your name?" Helen asks.

"Emmy."

"Well, Emmy, what would you like to see?"

"Bees. A giant one. My mum said all the bees are dying and they make flowers. My mum said the greedy bastards are killing them. I don't like bastards; they hurt bees."

Helen pauses, and tries not to laugh, but she quickly reads the room, and no one has batted an eyelid. *Is this acceptable language from a child in this town? Is this how her mother lets her express herself?* Emmy's twenty-five-year-old mum, in a tie dye dress and old cardigan, wearing work boots and a nose piercing, has a deadpan face and waits for Helen to respond.

But Ben from the Friday night discus-golf event counters with an offer. "I'll tell you what, Emmy. If you can make a giant bee, I'll put it way up in a tree for you. I'll put it up high, so if any of those naughty bastards try coming to our town, they will say, 'Whoa, I'm not going down there. They have giant bees in Wongii.'"

Emmy is very impressed with this and claps her hands. "Yeah. Mum, can we?"

"And we will take pictures, Emmy. LOTS of pictures." Helen returns her attention to the adults; it is back to all business. "We need to cover all social media platforms. They need to be competently updated, and we need volunteers for Instagram to post pics of the Festival Day, and it's lead up."

"I know people who can help with that," Emmy's mum assures her.

"And pics of Billy; his lead up, including his training."

"Don't get in Jack's way," Mr Exley warns.

"Oh!" Helen pauses. "Discreetly then. I'll coordinate a link between the new sites and Wongii's current website. And we need to keep track of any merchandise or art people are offering, or we are selling." Mr Exley and two others raise their hands. "Janine, you and I will start an official Billy Uke webpage."

Helen closes her laptop with a smile. "Thank you everyone. Thank you, Emmy. Let's get working."

*

Billy has been putting himself through the ringer. There are no jokes at training anymore, just the daunting reality of the task ahead. No down time, just exhaustion and sleep. And repetition. For the 100 m, 400 m, and hurdles, Jack has him concentrating on being quick off the mark. It entails a rigorous gym program of weighted squats and hopping, box jumping, single leg box jumps, hip thrusts, and a myriad more. Jack oversees everything, but most of the gym workout is delegated to Aaron, twice a day.

Jack reserves himself for the track and the finer details of pole vault, high and long jumps, discus, and javelin. But even away from the gym, Jack has Billy doing block starts into a sprint with a weighted vest on; 2 x 10 m block starts, 3 x 20 m, and 4 x 40m block starts, on top of endurance running. They don't have months to prepare … they have just seven weeks. And pressure is building.

Every time Billy jogs through town, someone is making a rubbish pile or cleaning their yard for the big day. His father has begun construction of the ring-toss deck, and two farmers dig post holes for him. Billy still thinks the whole thing is a bad idea. He doesn't want to go. And he has noticed people taking pictures of him, with their phones, as he runs through town.

When two people arrive and sat through long jumps, phones pointed at him, they keep their distance, and he puts up with it. But when the mat is out for pole vault training and a dozen people gather, it is a different matter. They talk, and move about for a better shot, and he is glad when Jack unceremoniously sends everyone packing.

But the art barn is a different story. He stops there. He has to. The children will not let him pass, wanting to show him the bees they are making. It begins with Emmy, some balloons, papier mâché, and some wire coat hangers. But Emmy has friends, and they have friends, and Billy watches the class grow to eighteen. It becomes a production line.

Additionally, Chris has been busy making bee frames with fencing wire and kids blow up balloons inside them. With the children's help, Ben mixes the papier mâché. Two hippie moms oversee the kids applying the mix. It is a long process for impatient kids who have to wait for things to dry. Wings have to be attached, and the painting done. They all want to show Billy where they are up to.

Chris invites Billy out the back of the barn to show him something. "Ben found out that four-year-old girls and eight-year-old boys are different."

Ben looks half asleep mixing papier mâché with a rake in a long feed trough. Globs of wet paper cling to his body, and small wads have dried in his curly hair. He stands in a patch of papier mâché snowballs the size of an eight-year-old's hand. The young culprits cackle at him from over the fence of a disused stock pen. "Shhh," Ben says. "Man, don't spook them."

*

Dividing her time between Sydney and Wongii has consumed Helen, but she has been ferocious in her effort. She has not forgotten about the bank; the bank has certainly not forgotten about her, and a relentless business energy is born.

For now, she has departmentalised the worry, segmented it off in her brain, and concentrated on a speedy design and registration of a Wongii logo. The contracts to join the Co-Op have been drawn up, subcommittees formed to put out festival flyers to neighbouring towns, posters have been printed, and she has searched regional and state offices for any grants available.

Helen has even made time to introduce herself at a council meeting in Clifton, the next town along, which is five times larger than Wongii and imperative as a potential customer for Wongii electricity.

A contract with them will make it easier to find investors.

Back in town, complaints of censorship have reached Janine from artists and the alternative quarter. At first, Janine and Helen dismiss them. But Mr Exley has called, alerting them to a potential disaster with the t-shirt sales, so Helen goes to the town hall to see for herself.

"What do we have?"

Mr Exley speaks to the artists, "Put on your creations and model for Helen."

The creators jump at the opportunity, slip on their shirts, and make a line. They all have the same thing on the back, 'Say no to drugs'. *Starting out well*, Helen thinks. The first model turns around to display Billy's face with the inscription: 'Wongii's own Drug Cheat.'.

"Ahh, no!" Exclaims Helen.

The next shirt, again with Billy's picture: 'Titan Drug Runner.'

"Take that off, please," declares Helen.

"Excuse me? Art is an expression of—" the creator and model begins.

"We will get sued for copyright infringement, using the word Titan. Take it off," she adds firmly. "Everyone! Turn around and show me what you have."

The remaining t-shirts read:

WANTED for Drug Running

Is He the Cheat?

More Drugs = Less Cheating

You really haven't thought this out too well, have you? She ponders, especially when she sees the last one. She massages her cheeks and purses her lips. "Nobody move," she advises.

Helen stands back with Mr Exley studying the shirts as if she is in a New York Art Gallery interpreting the conceptual magnitude of loneliness in a *Where's Wally* magazine. All of a sudden, she is in a hurry, searching around for a black marker pen. She finds one, strides forward, and begins crossing out words, replacing them with her own:

Is He the Cheat? became: Is Mother Nature a Cheat?

Wongii's Own Drug Cheat became: Wongii Cheats Drugs!

"Oooh! Ahh!" The models coo. Mr Exley strokes his chin, admiring her work as she returns alongside him to review the shirts.

To everyone's surprise, Mr Exley puts his hand out for the marker. She places it in his hand and he walks up to a model, scrubs out words to make space for his own, and returns. He puts the first two words above Billy's picture and the rest below:

More drugs = Less Cheating became: On Track! Are All Drugs Equal?

"Wow! Nice," admires Helen, also stroking her chin in critique. "It is less aggressive, more philosophical, with both a question and an answer. It even has direction! I think you have missed your calling in life, Mr Exley."

Mr Exley blushes to the sound of even louder coos: "Oh, Oh, Oh!"

"Oww, uh ha!"

"Yeah, yeah!" He tries to hide his grin as his model spins from side to side for the other models to see, showcasing the t-shirt as if it is his very own creation.

*

Totally committed and staying on task has left no room for doubt. But nerves have begun to creep in the night before. Over a wine at the breakfast counter, Helen has run through a festival checklist in her mind. She ticks boxes, runs through the time schedule, runs through 'what if' scenarios, and magically she is on her third glass, picking at the thread on her favourite jumper with no recollection of her second glass.

"I'm fretting again," she catches herself saying out loud. She tips the glass out and heads for a shower.

It is Thursday evening, and the festival is only two days away. She decides to leave in the morning for Wongii and get there a day early to check the progress and preparations—right after she calls Elliot.

Elliot is a peer and a friend from decades ago who moved to the US to start his own advertising company. He has landed some big contracts, established a thriving business, and sold the company for a fortune. He returned to Australia as a true success story. Elliot has contacts.

On the road into Wongii, the fretting and worry fall away. Helen has always found it scenic driving down the mountain and through the open fields, but this time turning the last real bend to approach the town, she feels inspired. Gumtrees house giant bees hovering over a branch in the breeze. Their black and orange bodies wobble about at the end of fencing wire, wrapped around the branches, in swarms of four or five.

"Awww," she sings to herself.

More are in the trees up ahead and she slows the car. Set back on the other side of the road, an old water tank has been painted as a beehive, with a dozen bees escaping, all on different lengths of wire. "Aww. Emmy, you are a genius."

Then the orange begins, and it did not seem to end. Helen rolls to a stop without pulling over. "Ah!" Every house in town has been painted orange. The few that have not fully participated have at least painted their doors and windowsills orange. Wongii sits looking rather ridiculous in the valley.

Tentatively, she continues to the Wongii Hotel. It appears to be a two-tone town of orange: there is orange, and there is a watered-down orange. The car park is full of cars and trucks, but it now has a pen of nannie goats built along the back fence.

Dressed for business, Helen gets out of her car and grabs her suit bag and luggage from the back seat. Turning around, she is momentarily stunned as she stares up at the bright orange pub; it is the colour of a newly bought tractor.

"Good god."

The public bar is empty except for one, and he is asleep at the table amongst a pile of dirty glasses. There is no one behind the bar either.

"An empty bar in Wongii? Unusual to say the least," she says to herself. "But then again, the town is orange."

She knows her way around the pub. This is where she stayed when working in Wongii, and her room key will be in the Lounge Bar. But there is no one in there either, just some noise coming from the street. She places her luggage and suit bag on the staircase leading up to the accommodation and goes to investigate.

Helen opens the Lounge Bar entrance door to a marmalade eyesore busy with people in festival setup. The street looks like Picasso and Van Gough have been on a bender with Keith Richards and Iggy Pop. Brightly painted canvas stalls are being erected, weird sculptures stand by, ugly windmills spin, and a truck passes by with a huge misshapen clown head on a pole. All against an orange backdrop.

Art is everywhere, and just about everything is made from recycled materials. Helen is gobsmacked. She looks up to find a female transformer standing over her; it appears to have been built from farm parts and old machinery. Helen thinks it is a complete artistic failure with its milk tin breasts, cow teat sucker tassels hanging from them, black garden rake eyelashes, puffy inner tube red lips, and carrying a parasol made from a clothesline. Transfixed on the breasts and tassels, she thinks it far closer to a drag queen or stripper than a transformer.

"Feminist statement or fashion statement? I hope to bring attention to why there are so many Male Transformers," the artist declares as she begins rolling up a lead, still with the welding mask on her head.

Helen's mind goes blank. She doesn't quite know how to reply.

A man walks by with an orange splattered tarp. "This ought to get some attention." He grins eagerly. "And it was cheap! It turns out no one bids for orange paint online."

"Yes," Helen nods hesitantly, "Yes, I imagine so."

Further along, there is a short-legged elephant made of a variety of different sized tires, and she can see Emmy and a friend playing there. An older Koori kid lifts the elephant's trunk and feeds it some apples. Emmy and her friend catch them as they roll out its bum, and take a bite, giggling as little girls do.

"Don't fret," she steadies herself. "Don't over analyse. What's done is done. Too late to change things now." She runs after the transformer artist, packing her truck.

"Excuse me? Do you have a spare work shirt I could borrow?"

"Yes. I do."

She gets to work with the townsfolk and works till well after dark. A late meal and a couple of drinks with the locals afterwards, sees Helen drop off to sleep with no time to worry.

CHAPTER 4

IT ONLY TAKES sunrise to make the town vivid … the orange sun plays on orange houses. But festival day brings balloons, clowns, face painting for children, and people in crazy costumes walking around on stilts, as well. The face painting is not just for kids. Many of the alternative people have turned up with their faces already painted or glittered, and they wear loud, colourful clothes to complete the picture.

Vans full of hippies arrive from other communities and if they don't have flowers in their hair, the designs are painted on their vans and skin.

People from Clifton also arrive, and soon buy t-shirts to replace the ones they came in. Billy's face is everywhere. And of course, art—stalls sell pottery, sculptures, and paintings.

Janine takes pictures of kids hurling hoops from Laddie's deck onto short multi-coloured fence posts. Odd, homemade stuffed toys and showbags sit beneath each post. Hoops fly, or in some cases roll, to their destinations, falling over posts and prizes close enough together to give the smallest of kids a chance. But Helen is too busy checking her messages to notice. She looks up to see Janine scowling at her.

"Oh, I was hoping to hear from Elliot," she says. "He has serious connections. He's green, health conscious … Wongii would be a good fit. You would like him. He is even a patron of the World Animal Protection Society."

"You're right, I like him already. But he's not here," points out Janine. "Relax, okay? You have done all you can do. For someone promoting healthy living …?"

"You're right."

Helen can see the massive Picasso clown head on a post and decides to give that her attention. It must have been dropped on the truck tray when still wet to get that split, disjointed effect. Now reinforced and painted over, it looks priceless. Rotating on the post with a gaping open mouth, contestants stand around shooting basketballs into it. Those that don't go in the mouth bounce off wildly in unpredictable directions and often hit walkers strolling by or other contestants about to take a shot.

The stoner running the show doesn't care. He has had what he called Molly's breakfast: a healthy, hearty meal, followed by a little MDMA. Not enough to interfere with smoking a joint before he faces the crowd, but enough to top off the coffee. If six people pay at once, they all get three balls. There is only one clown head. It isn't his problem that there are so many people. He just walks around in a circle with a shopping trolley full of balls to sell.

Janine and Helen wander along to find Mary Uke admiring a sculpture and stop to say hello. The sculpture is titled *ELEVATION*. Janine reads aloud the inscription underneath: 'Sport above reproach. Two minds locked in battle, above outside influence.'

Two tennis umpire chairs are welded together face-to-face, and a chessboard is welded onto the armrests between the seating, relegating them to no more than adult high chairs. They are wobbly and difficult to climb, but people are paying to play a game and have their picture taken in the interactive art and with its creator. Two men squirm as they played, legs uncomfortably tangled between pipes and each other.

Laddie Uke is tugging on one man's leg, querying: "Are you winning?" And then to the other: "What about you, you winning?"

"Piss off Laddie."

He starts jumping up and down to get a better look. "What's the score?" Mary starts to cackle.

"C'mon Laddie, I'm working here," Julian, the sculptor, moves in on Laddie, and escorts him back to Mary. "Take him home, would you?"

Helen becomes aware that she is at ease, laughing along with Mary and Janine. Looking around, she sees stilt walkers with long noses passing, and kids with ice cream. It all makes her feel lighter. It has been so long since she'd stopped thinking and just laughed.

People are gravitating towards the back of the pub, so they follow along. A crowd that is four-deep had gathered around the goat pen, and people are hanging over the fence with their phones out. Phones out themselves, Helen and Janine approach the fence and people make room for them to get to the front. They stop to watch a passing goat as it pauses right in front of Helen. The top of its head is dyed bright pink; it has sparkly earrings dangling and is wearing a sports bra. It gets chased off by a nannie goat in suspenders.

Helen recoils a step and puts her head in her hands. "Oh, God. This is so bad," she mutters.

Janine gives a devilish laugh. "This is my dad and Uncle Dale." She points across the pen, declaring, "Look upon my childhood."

A large painted sheet of plywood reads: 'Celebrity Goat Naming $100. $250 for first impregnated.'

A second sheet is divided into twenty available spaces and every one of them has been filled with a name. None of the flock has been spared. Garter belts and boas adorn half the pen. There are even short skirts and padded bras, veils, red blushed cheeks, and two of the goats are wearing corsets. The goats themselves seem happy enough roving about taste-testing the fashion from whomever is standing still. Each goat wears their sponsor's celebrity name tag instead of a number.

Jack has been taking side bets, offering ten times your money if you can pick which one of the celebrities his prized cashmere buck,

Sir Linneaus, gets to first. He is now standing tall and proud with Sir Linneaus, who is modelling at the gate. Meanwhile, Emmy's mum is taking pictures.

Helen can only imagine how many pictures have already been taken of the flock. She gives in and takes her place at the front of the fence alongside Janine, "Just don't get any photos with me in them."

Jack slips a studded black leather cap on Sir Linneaus, as Dale climbs up the first rail of the pen and pulls out a microphone. "Ladies and gentlemen, and all others of any description, I present to you our very own Sir Linneaus."

Jack opens the gate, and the buck jumps forward. The crowd lets out a cheer.

"The wonderful Sir Linneaus," Dale chortles. "Ladies and … oh, oh, oh! He's wasting no time, is he? Rushing to Madonna—*Like A Virgin* Madonna, only to be run off by Billie Eilish."

Nannies jostle about the pen trying to get away. In chorus, but no harmony, the crowd "Oohs" in anticipation of, and then "Aahhs" with disappointment.

"—who is rejected for Scarlett Johansson's Black Widow," Dale's voice intones. "Nope, she proves far too much for him. Intimidated by a strong, independent female, he moves on to Hillary Clinton, people. And he walks right on by her. Right on by like she wasn't even there. Brutal."

Hellen can't help but break out laughing at Dale's commentary. "But Kylie Minogue, JLo, and Freddie Mercury are starting to strut their stuff. Gooo Freddyyyy," Dale calls long.

The "Oohs" and the "Aahs" of the crowd grow with each new impending impregnation until it becomes its own game. Janine and Helen are red with laughter.

"They are strutting their stuff out front for Sir Linneaus … Wait, there is a Kardashian in the field, people, a Kardashian! Is modification allowed or is this blatant performance enhancement before our very eyes? Tough question. Even tougher when there is a second

Kardashian, and you can't tell them apart. But it matters no more because here she is, ladies and gentlemen, Janis is here. Janis Joplin, with a classic feathered boa, is rocking the world of Sir Linneus. Go Janis Go."

The crowd "Ooh," and "Aah" again in anticipation, until the final "Ooh" erupts into hollering catcalls and applause.

Janine laughs even harder when she sees Helen averting her eyes and looking away from the actual goat sex.

CHAPTER 5

THE FOLLOWING DAY, Jack, Janine, Dale and his constant companion, Rubi, and Helen are enjoying the quieter surroundings and a bite to eat on the Buckman veranda. They all have the takings from one event or another and Rubi is trying to eat Dale's shoe laces. Helen is relieved it is all finally being put together.

Dale peeks into Janine's paper bag. "Is all that from the art money?"

"Yes. But second and third place donated the money back to Billy."

"What about first place?" Jack enquires.

"Dad?" She warns.

"Cheap bastard."

"Happy thoughts, Father, happy thoughts."

Helen's phone rings. She sees the name Elliot and her voice becomes business like. "Excuse me, I should take this." She strides across the yard for privacy.

"Elliot, how are you?" Half cheery and half sales.

"I chair a committee that liberates performing bears from shackles. And you ask my help, while tarting up goats as prostitutes?" Elliot's voice is controlled, slow, and deliberate.

Helen is mortified. For a moment she cannot speak, "No. No, that wasn't me."

"Your handiwork is all over the internet. What on earth were you thinking?"

A hot flush of humiliation races and settles tingling in her hairline. Desperate, she tries to explain. "I had no control. That was the Wongii Fundraising—"

"They were GAMBLING ON ANIMAL SEX, HELEN!" He explodes, cutting her off. "With a goat dressed as a Girl Scout, for fuck's sake."

"That was Taylor Swift."

"Oh. I'm sure she appreciates that."

"No one really takes dress ups seriously."

"Have you even heard of transgender? My—" he stops. There is a long, ugly silence. "You know what? Don't call again, Helen." He hangs up.

"Elliot? Elliot?!" She squirms in anxiety. "Shit. Shit." She twists and wriggles in anguish. With her feet planted firmly in a paddock, she looks like an introvert dragged out and forced onto the dancefloor.

Compose yourself, breathe. Breathe, he is just one investor.

Helen puts her phone away and steadies herself. Crossing the yard, she returns to the veranda finding Dale waiting at the top of the steps.

"Everything alright, dear?"

"Fine." She is curt and annoyed. "Just business."

"Well, how is this for business? Sir Linneaus certainly did his bit." Jovially, Jack hands over a paper bag of money.

"He certainly did," retorts Helen dryly before opening the bag. Looking inside though, she is genuinely impressed. Her tone is much warmer as she states, "Well done, gentlemen. How much is here?"

"$1,750.00 from the goat naming, and $2,400 from the betting," Dale informs her proudly.

"Okay then. How is it being divided?" Asks Janine, appearing beside him. "How many and who is going?"

"Well, I'm really not happy with the coverage we got. The press was non-existent. I think I need to stay and—" Helen began explaining.

"Oh no," Janine jumped in. "We are not leaving Billy alone with Dad. Not in Cuba. Not without supervision."

"Oh, I'm not going. Too hot for me." Jack poured water on the idea.

"What do you mean, you're not going? You have to go. You are his coach." Helen is flabbergasted.

"He'll need a friend more than he needs a coach." Jack motions his head towards Billy and Aaron in the paddock. Aaron is down low at the sandbox inspecting Billy's action as he launches into a long jump. "Billy just needs reminding, that's all. Besides, do you really want it to be me fronting the media for you?"

"Wellll ..." Janine draws out. "That's decided then, isn't it?" She is fully onboard with Jack being kept away from the media as she winks at Helen.

"We still have a medical side to cover. It's not like we have insurance, and another team is not going to lend us a doctor." Helen declares wanting all bases covered.

"Ask Manohar," prompts Jack.

"He is our yoga instructor in Wongii," Dale adds. "And he makes the best herbal teas. Manohar works as a physiotherapist in Clifton, a couple of days a week. He's always fixing the boys up after injury."

And just like that, the away team is decided: Billy, Helen, Aaron, and Manohar are going to be taking on 'the world'.

*

Billy thinks a sendoff is totally unnecessary after a festival. He's already had too much fanfare and does not need the pressure. Still, with the Buckmans and Dale, the Uke extended family, Manohar and family, plus a few selected locals and their kids, who had devoted much time and effort to Billy, they make up quite a gathering.

A spread of healthy food is laid out on the tables set out on the lawn. Emmy and some kids are playing 'chasings' around the house, and Aaron has some ten-year-olds on the track. They run long jumps into the sand at one end, and he has the mat laid out for high jumps, on the other side.

Jack, Dale and Rubi, and Laddie are drinking beer on the veranda, but Helen suddenly notices that Billy is nowhere to be seen. Before she can ask Janine or search for herself, Janine introduces Manohar to her.

"I can't thank you enough for joining the team at such short notice. Especially with a family," states Helen, shaking Manohar's hand. Manohar's wife is talking to Mary Uke, and his two daughters are running around with Emmy.

Manohar has a dignified and very gentle nature about him. As an Australian/Indian Sikh, of thirty-five years old, he is a man of aver age height, and is fit-looking. Helen thinks he is strikingly handsome.

"Oh, not at all. It's a wonderful adventure. Plus, if you take Billy and Aaron's injuries away, that is half my business," he jokes.

"Oh, it's been like that, has it?" Helen jokes back.

Janine nods, grinning.

"And Guantanamo has always been such a secretive place. Google Maps draws a blank. The only pictures I've seen are inside the stadium."

"Well, we have a brochure of the facilities and accommodation. I'll just be a moment," replies Helen, and heads across the yard to the house to retrieve it.

*

"Our little town has really pulled together. They've done well," Laddie says, admiring the gathering from the veranda.

"Pfff. It looks like a marmalade sandwich," Jack scoffs. "Half of them are lost and bickering, and the others run around like headless chooks."

"You really can be a cantankerous old bastard," Laddie remarks.

"He was cantankerous when we wore flowers in our hair," Dale comments as if it is obvious.

"But Billy has all the lost chickens running in the same direction now. Have you ever tried to stop a flock of chickens?" Jack sweeps his hand across the yard.

Jack takes a seat by the doorway to roll a cigarette, leaving Laddie proud. He looks up to see Helen crossing the yard. He watches as Emmy, and three other four-and five-year-olds come racing around the side of the house and almost run into her. One cries out in surprise, and Helen spinning around, growls out, "Rahr," pretending to 'get them'.

The little girls let out a high-pitched scream, and Rubi drops like a stone at Jack's feet. He looks down at her and shakes his head in disgust. Helen is still shading her eyes, and her lips relax into a contented, mirthful grin as she watches the kids run away.

Jack lifts his head and lights his smoke as Helen cheerfully climbs the stairs. She exchanges a pleasant smile with Jack and carefully steps past Rubi, thinking she is asleep.

Jack returns his gaze to Rubi and shakes his head in disgust, again.

*

Helen enters the kitchen looking for her bag with the brochure, and finds Billy there, scrolling through his phone.

"Shouldn't you be out enjoying the party?"

"You know we are going to look like fools, don't you?" He doesn't lift his head, just his eyes.

Oh, oh! " That's just nerves," Helen consoles him.

"It's not nerves. It's the drugs. You have no idea how much difference they make," he sighs.

"From what I hear, you may be underestimating yourself," she tries again.

Billy shakes his head, dismissing this as nonsense. Sulkily, he saunters off.

Helen hesitates a second, thinking quickly about how she should handle this. She knows that she has to follow him.

"And the Grasshopper?" Billy spins around to meet her.

She stares blankly at him. She has no idea what he is talking about. He thrusts his phone at her. On screen, there is a man with curly dark hair and nine medals around his neck. The image doesn't help; she doesn't recognise him as she doesn't follow sports. She wants to scream, "Ah, c'mon, it's the DECATHLON!" But she knows this would likely flip his mood ... in the wrong direction.

"The Decathlon Legend ..." he hints. "... coming out of retirement for these games?"

Helen is still stumped.

Rolling his eyes, he waves her away, and goes over to talk to people who at least know about the Grasshopper.

She goes to stride after him, but on opening the screen door to the veranda, Billy is already appealing to his father, Jack, and Dale.

"I can't do this," she hears him pleading. "I can't think of one event I even have a chance in. And there are ten."

"Ha!" Jack lets out a boisterous laugh. "You haven't got a hope in hell of winning an event. Get that right out of your head."

"Are you still looking for ribbons, son?"

It is not the response Billy wants, and it is certainly not the one he envisaged. He flounders without an answer.

"No one is asking you to win anything. That's you." Laddie looks deep into his son's eyes. "People are just asking you to carry their name."

"I said you could hold your own against cheating bastards, and you can. I know what you're capable of, and you can stay up better than halfway. That's enough to give people something to talk about. Everyone will be souped up on steroids BUT you. You're the standout." Jack's voice is calm and full of confidence.

"Exactly! Validity!" Helen bursts into the conversation from the doorway. "It is not about who beats you. It is about how many athletes on steroids you beat." She strides out, becoming enthusiastic and excited. "With organic food! Think about that. It puts the whole drug thing into question. There is a lot of spin and advertising for Wongii out of that, Billy."

Billy stares at everyone, finally beginning to process everything and connecting the dots. It wasn't all about him. One of those dots was his hometown. Friends would soon lose their jobs and be forced to move on. The town would die. He didn't object to the logic, but it did not allay his fears at all.

"Baaaaaaa," Rubi wakes and nudges Helen, who is standing next to her.

"Oh, hi Rubi," she pats Rubi and lets Billy mull it over.

Jack groans heavily. He turns up his lip and looks away.

CHAPTER 6

THEY FLY FROM Sydney, Australia to Santiago, Chile, in South America. They go via Auckland, New Zealand. It is a three-hour flight, followed by eleven more. Helen books overnight accommodation in Santiago.

There are daily flights to Cuba from there, but you cannot enter Guantanamo Bay from Cuba. Even the Cubans cannot do that. The pharmaceutical companies that run the Titan Games all have their businesses in the US, and every one of them is scared of breaking the US embargo. All competitors have been warned that stopping there would have you disqualified from the Games. The US Military still insist they owned 'the Bay'.

Early the next morning, they fly another six hours and fifty minutes to Panama City. It's an hour's wait between flights, and then they board their final plane for Kingston, Jamaica, two hours away. From there, they will travel by ship to Guantanamo Bay.

Disembarking at Kingston Airport, and worn out with jet lag, the Wongii Team make their way up the long wide hallway until they came to a divided doorway. Helen reads the sign above the doorway and looks back to their tickets. She is unsure which way to go. The sign above her reads:

'WELCOME TITANS.
All contraband for Guantanamo Bay bypass
Customs. Please stay left.
All others, go right to collect your baggage.'

But there is another big bright sign to the left, above a refreshment table of drinks and moist towels for Titans, that reads:

'Your Baggage, Drugs and Supplements are
loaded directly to your private jets courtesy of
YIELD Sports Supplements...

YIELD— Providing Foreign Aid you can see!'

No one said anything about a private jet, so Helen goes right.

It is not a huge airport like London or New York and the baggage carousels are, thankfully, close by. Aaron and Billy wanted to eat, and Helen wants a nap. They collect their bags and stand in line for customs and inspection. Through the wall-sized windows they can see the commotion of a protest taking place outside, with people waving placards: *Lift the Embargo! 62 years is long enough!*

But they are also protesting the Titan Games: Military + Pharmaceuticals = Bad Medicine. They watch, wide-eyed, as a woman is dragged out of the airport wearing a t-shirt with these same words. She refuses to use her legs so that the security guards earn their money. An officer rolls his eyes when they put her down, as if it has become a daily routine that he is far from happy with.

The line moves fast as people with nothing to declare run their bags through the x-ray machine. Having to declare goods, they wait until a space is available, and an officer beckons them across.

Manohar plonks the suitcase full of food on the table first, unzips the flap, and pulls it back for inspection. A young officer begins his duties on the bag as Helen presents passports and papers to the senior customs officer; she is a fifty-year-old lady, behind a computer. The senior officer takes one look at the paperwork and hands it all, passports included, back to Helen. The younger officer stops and flips the suitcase flap closed.

"We cannot look in a Titan's bag. Guantanamo is contractually exempt from customs. Go back around to your friends," she advises and points outside.

Manohar looks outside at the melee taking place. "Oh, no," he states, shaking his head and opening the bags again, "We have rice and pasta to declare. We have—"

"Leave the bag shut unless you want to be arrested," she declares sternly. "Your contraband is illegal on this side of the terminal, sir. Return immediately. Your jet awaits you."

"We have no contraband, officer. We are organic. And no fresh produce. We need to buy that here," interjected Helen. "Nor do we have a jet waiting. Our tickets are to board a passenger ship called the *SS Stewie*, from Annotto Bay. I was under the impression everyone, Titans that is, were to board that ship."

The officer stretches her hand out and takes the paperwork back. A cynical half smile appears as she reads the ticket. "There is no passenger ship from anywhere on the planet to Guantanamo Bay." She bangs her fingers on the keyboard stating, "I smell a rat. There are only private jets cleared by the US and …" she pauses. "Aah, here we are. You are on a supply vessel."

"Oh, I really don't like boats," Manohar's face drops. "I thought it was like a cruise ship or a large passenger ferry."

Helen is puzzled. She was under the same impression.

The senior officer turns to her partner, smiling, "And there are a lot more protesters in Cuba. It is just the fence is bigger, eh?" She jokes.

More relaxed, she turns to Helen. "The blockade has prevented Cuba from having pesticides for forty years. It has since become the organic food hub of the Caribbean. Not all appreciate this. You will find fresh produce in Annotto Bay. But you will find none where you are going." She passes the paperwork back to Helen and clears them with a grin. "Good luck."

They collect their luggage and make their way out of the airport, where buses and taxis are waiting. They still need to get to Annotto Bay; it is two hours away.

"You don't like boats, Manohar? You will be fine, it's only five hours. I'll get you some patches."

*

The team stay overnight in Annotto Bay in the mixture of sleep and wake that only jet lag can give.

After breakfast, they ask the staff for directions to the market. They ready their bags and leave them in storage behind the front desk. Vacating their rooms, they set out.

Thankfully, fresh produce is readily available, just as the customs officer had assured. It is a bonus that the organic vegetables and fruit are acquired at a price that surprises them. It is inexpensive compared to the supermarkets in Australia. There are even fruits and vegetables they had not tried or seen before. An ice cold, blended guanabana soon becomes Aaron's favourite.

A week's worth of produce is packed into a crate, and they return by taxi to the hotel for their luggage. A second taxi is needed to ferry them all, plus the crate and bags, to the dock. Once tickets and passports are checked, they board the 40-metre supply vessel and stow their crate and luggage just inside a hatchway, stacked high to save room.

The *SS Stewie* is not set up for passengers at all. Ropes and cables hold down cargo and run across sections of the deck, making them a no-go zone for anyone other than the crew. The best that the Wongii Troupe can do is stay out of the way, on the few seats available on the back deck.

Billy and Aaron lean against the rails on the port side, admiring the clear waters of the Caribbean for the first time. Annotto Bay begins to slip away behind them; it is a beautiful day, and adventure lies ahead.

Manohar and Helen's body clocks have not yet recovered from jet lag, and they sit back in their seats, relaxing.

A loud crash causes Helen to jump as a small trash bin comes flying by, rubbish scattering everywhere. Yelling escalates. A woman storms after it and kicks it again. She is thick set with broad shoulders but is no taller than Helen. Her Union Jack t-shirt is dark with perspiration under her arms, and beads of sweat pool on her brow beneath a purple mohawk.

"We couldn't find you for thirty-six hours." A skinny, much older manager chases after her. "The jet is in the Cayman Islands now. There is nothing I could do."

"Along with my fucking stash!" The accent is distinctly Northern English. "It should be part of my bloody diet by now, not with some idiot doctor. Fuuuuck." she screams at the sea.

Manohar does his best to avoid eye contact, but the scene is playing out right in front of him. He turns in his seat, diverting his attention to Helen, and passes on the receipts from the organic produce shopping. "I have arranged for the same food order to be delivered weekly."

"Whuah," Helen pukes. It is short and sharp and lands on the deck between them all. The colour drains from her face, leaving it grey with the onslaught of seasickness.

Among the onlookers—that shared reflex people have with vomit of turning one's nose up and holding lips tightly shut, whether it be in disgust or sympathy—takes hold. It is momentary paralysis.

The smell carries in the breeze, and the English Punk gags on it. Before Helen can get to her feet, it starts again.

The second vomit comes with sound effects in a long, drawn out, proper seasick hurl. The ferocity of its beginning alone is the stuff of nightmares, and it makes the English Punk gag again. But this time her back lurches into it, forcing her to cover her mouth.

Helen's vomit splashes across the deck and the regurgitated scrambled eggs are too much for the Punk to take. She gags again, succumbing to it, and vomit splays out between her fingers. She spins away towards the sea, gripping onto the rails, and heaves profusely overboard.

Aaron grabs the bin and shoves it in front of Helen. She lets fly again and barfs into it. "Whuuurk." The sound echoes out of the empty chamber. The Punk turns back around at the sound, sees what is in the bucket, and begins again with gusto. Seasickness has set in, and so it goes over the next couple of hours.

*

The arrival into Guantanamo Bay is a spectacular sight that Helen does not get to enjoy.

The Titan Games are set beneath a jungle-covered mountain that tightly wraps around the complex. The crystal-clear waters and white sands of the bay would match any of the most popular tourist destinations in the world. Tropical greenery and coconut trees give way to manicured lawns and gardens and run back to sporting practice fields and new residential buildings.

The main stadium is set way back and stands out like a modern-day colosseum. The stadium building appears all the more impressive as it is surrounded by trees, recreation parks, and practice fields, instead of car parks and train lines.

Excitement creeps into Billy. He wants to see more.

A courtesy bus awaits to take both parties to their respective residential blocks. The Titan Punk has the back seat to herself; her manager sits two seats away relieved her drugs are not far away.

Billy sits forward in his seat, roused from the arduous three or four-day trek to get here … he is unsure of how long it has taken, with the constant time changes.

The bus winds its way around hustling hockey fields; short, red, six-laned practice tracks that are scattered around the area with sand boxes or high jump mats at the end. There are nets already hung for discus and hammer throw practice; modern complexes for gymnasiums, swimming, and diving; and bikes whizzing in and out of a steep, covered, cycling velodrome. They also fly past onto the road, shooting by the courtesy bus.

Behind Billy, a washed-out Helen cradles her head, dreaming of a toothbrush. She squints. *That sun hurts.*

*

The attention to detail and craftsmanship exudes from the exquisite, 17th century French rosewood desk. It sits in a vast office with Mr Weeks sitting behind it, immaculate as always.

Fifty-three years old, suave, and well spoken, he is a light-framed 175 cm; he has no interest in fitness or working out. He pays more attention to his skin.

The desk is of a considerable size, as is the matching, high-backed viscount chair, but Mr Weeks seems to fit them well and looks very comfortable.

"The sponsors expect all attention to be on THEIR products. Not this guy, or whatever he is peddling. He does not fit. He is not to be seen or heard. Understood?" Mr Weeks passes a file with a picture of Billy inside to Mr Daniel, the Security Chief. "And as discreetly as possible, please."

"Is it some kind of protest run?" Mr Daniel cannot hide that he is ex-military; it is in his every movement. Forty-four, with grey flecks on the sides of his dark hair, he is extremely fit, 181 cm, and disciplined.

"Let's just say that I pay you to keep the politics out of sport, shall we?" Mr Weeks pauses for a moment. He is holding a file with a picture of Helen attached to it. "I see Ms Helen Ellis is already in some financial difficulty with her house. I should be able to nip this in the bud."

*

The team struggle with the excess baggage of Billy's equipment, a suitcase of organic food, and now a box of fresh produce, from the bus into the foyer. The security guard at the desk does not offer to help, nor does he wait for Helen to introduce herself. He simply handed her a swipe card, and states, "Ground floor."

Aaron and Billy take their bags into the hallway and return for the crate. Manohar ferries the bags further along as Helen wheels her own suitcase to locate the room. She unlocks the door, pushes it open, and enters. She stands aghast at how small the accommodation is; it becomes a lot smaller still when the others follow suit.

They are in the central room, and all it has is a kitchenette with a fridge and a table for two. The four 'bedrooms' were once military prison cells, and not much has changed: 3 x 2 metres or 9 x 6 feet. The beds are bolted against the wall, and after a small set of drawers were added to the room, there is not enough space to open a door, so the doors had all been removed.

The only door is to the one bathroom they will all have to share, and it is through the kitchenette. The place is ridiculous.

"This can't be right," Helen croaks, as Billy drops his bag and scoffs.

"It doesn't quite look like the brochure, does it?" Sniffs Manohar.

"Can we eat? I'm starving," Aaron asks.

"God, I just want a shower. I couldn't eat. I will inquire about the room though, once I've showered, I promise," Helen assures.

"You need to rehydrate. And eat a little something if you can. I will put some food together and we can eat at the cafeteria. Let Helen shower." Manohar opens the suitcase of food from home, pulls out a Wongii-made, pastel-flowered hamper bag for lunches during training, and fills it with an evening meal. The three of them set off to find the cafeteria.

*

The complex is well signed, and it is easy to find the cafeteria.

Checking out the general layout and passing so many people of different nationalities along the way rekindles a spark in the men; they soon forget about the absurd accommodation. Yet they cannot forget their hunger and they are glad to reach their destination.

Seeing the cafeteria doorways hustle with the comings and goings of teams and entourages, they are eager to join them, and Aaron leads the way.

Loud and alive, the cafeteria does not disappoint.

From all walks of life, pockets of people sit in colourful groups. There are tracksuits in national colours, traditional clothing worn proud, pharmaceutical logos blazed across tracksuits and t-shirts, and men in suits looking out of place and odd. But it is the athletes themselves that stand out the most. The Titans are mixed amongst the different pockets. They stand out freakish or too perfect; too tall, too muscular, too hairy, too much protruding jaw, bright braces on their teeth with under bites you could drop a coin in. They are daunting.

A slightly built man in a Swedish tracksuit scrapes part of his meal into a bin alongside Manohar. He is being very meticulous about what stays and what goes, muttering away to himself, "Too many beans, bad, bad not even. Too many. Not even. Where are the carrots?"

Manohar scowls at the antics of the twenty-five-year-old, puzzled.

Green 'Gotta-Aid' bottles dot every table from the mezzanine to the lower level.

There isn't a servery counter or servery staff, only cleaners.

Automatic Teller Machine-like vending machines have replaced the traditional food servery. They run along the length of the wall and hooks around to the next one. Each outlet competes with the other and bears the beaming brand name of its pharmaceutical company sponsor. Each meal tray that is dispensed is carefully prepared for each individual competitor down to the kilojoules, the vitamins, the nutrients, the hormones, the steroids, and the uppers.

Aaron pulls his phone out for a pic. "Oh, Mum will love this," he says sarcastically.

They are close enough to the first two machines to witness them in action when an extremely tall Englishmen is at one and a smallish South Korean at the other.

The Englishman taps his card, as one would a visa card, and an announcement begins: "Welcome Tom Walsh. Your meal has been approved by Forever Pharmaceuticals. We go on, and on, and on."

The South Korean does the same: "Welcome Han-Gyeol Kyung. Your meal has been approved by Forever Pharmaceuticals. We go on and on and on."

A sealed meal and cutlery slide out to a bench, and the Englishman picks them up and departs. When the South Korean picks up his sealed meal, Aaron and Billy are astounded at the size of the man's hands. Not just huge hands or oversized, these are enormous, dinner-plate palmed, cucumber-fingered, gigantism injected, shocking hands. So much so that he fumbles dreadfully at picking up the chopsticks from a flat surface. He tries again. He fails. He tries again and fails. He tries sweeping his fingers across them slowly to pick them up lengthways. He fails. Changing his stance, he tries again …

"Look, Bill. Even Mickey Mouse is here," Aaron chuckles, pointing with his lips at the man's hands.

"Nah, Mickey Mouse was a Blackfella." Billy is categorical about it. "He just wore those weird, white, minstrel gloves later on in his career. In his first film, *Steamboat Willy*, he doesn't wear any gloves. And his working hands are black!"

"Holy shit." Aaron takes a moment and squints a little taking it all in. "Let's get you out of here before an American hears you talk like that. We're not in Wongii now. What the fuck's wrong with you?" He pushes Billy along in search of a table.

The place is full, especially on this level, and as they walk around looking for a spot to eat, they are happy to find a table of fellow Australians that has empty seats.

"Hey, some Aussies," Billy declares. They walk to the table and introduce themselves.

"Hello, I am Manohar. And we are—" Manohar begins.

"Oh, we know who you are," the Australian manager motions towards the Wongii logo on the pastel-flowered hamper bag.

Manohar smiles, "Oh, yes. Mind if we join you?"

"Yes. Yes, I do mind."

Manohar is taken aback. No one looks up from the table. No one speaks either, not even amongst themselves.

"Is there some sort of problem?" he asks.

"We are on the same team, you know," says Billy.

"You are not on our 'team'," the man growls at Billy. "You are on your own." He returns his attention to Manohar and points to the Wongii hamper box with his fork. "This is business, and you have no business being here."

Billy and Manohar don't know what to say. They are shocked. But Aaron bristles at the man's smugness. He kicks at the leg of an athlete's chair. "And what have you got to say?"

The man looks up. "I can't say anything, mate. I'm under contract."

Aaron holds his eyes until the man concedes and returns to his meal. "No words. No manners," Aaron asks the rest of the table. "Just contracts?"

"Come away Aaron." Manohar sees a glimpse of Jack in Aaron, and it worries him. "There is nothing but bad karma at this table."

They leave the table, and that level, and take the stairs downwards.

*

Helen manages to eat some fruit after her rejuvenating shower, but it feels claustrophobic eating it in the prisonlike space. She has made a promise about the rooms, and so she sets out for the front desk. She thinks she needs the air, anyway.

"Could I speak to somebody about the rooms, please?"

"We are security, madame. That is something you will have to take up with admin." He is rigid, if not stern.

"Okay. Well, where could I find our allocated massage table? Every room is supposed to have one," Helen tests him.

"Admin is located four blocks down, madame."

She decides not to waste any more time with them and leaves the building looking for someone who can help.

Helen locates the Administration Office at the end of the residential blocks, where the practice fields begin. Facing the stadium, there is a small park with trees and benches directly opposite. The air is refreshing, and Helen enjoys the walk. *I can smell the ocean,* she muses. Unfortunately, the office is closed, and no one is inside.

The Media Centre alongside, however, is buzzing with activity. She looks closer and thinks that there are plenty of Administration Officers in there. She walks towards the door, but a security guard stops her. He shut her down before she can even speak. "Admin is closed, madame. Come back tomorrow."

She thinks the security guards' repetition is robotic. With a set jaw, she points towards the admin staff inside the media centre.

"Not unless you have been issued a Press Badge. Have you been issued one?"

She doesn't bother with any further discussion and retreats to the park. She sits on the bench and watches the action in the Media Centre. *Something is not right.*

Her phone beeps with a message from Aaron. She opens it but is a little puzzled by what she sees. It is a picture of some sort of ATM machine but with a pharmaceutical logo instead of a bank logo. *Is that a drug dispenser?!*

*

Billy and Aaron eat in silence, brooding. Manohar is reading the contents of a Gotta Aid bottle. At first, he looks perplexed, then concerned, and suddenly, he puts the bottle down quickly, wiping his hands afterwards as if he has been handling poison. He can't help but hear the conversation at the table alongside him.

"Vegetarians are unnatural! Whey powder alone will always require drugs to compete," an Italian trainer argues.

"Yes. Man is omnivore," agrees an over muscled, and overly hairy Greek athlete. "Crushed seahorse for creatine, and bovine protein for me. It is far more natural."

"Can you believe those guys?" Billy breaks the quiet.

"Arseholes. All of them," Aaron counters.

"Fuck off, Calculus, I'm eating." A broad Scottish accent rises above the drone of the room from four tables down. He is huge, bearded, and angry, and has five meal trays in front of him over which he hovers, like a lion does with a kill from hyenas.

"Not even. Not even," explains the guy in the Swedish tracksuit, as he continues to rearrange chairs. He takes a chair from the Scotsman's table and places it at another. He moves on to count the chairs at the next table, making sure there is an even number. He then looks back ominously to the five dinner trays in front of the Scotsman. "Not even."

The Italian trainer leans into the Wongii table and twirls his finger at his temple. "He is from the DJ/Chess Squad," he explains in what appears to be a sympathetic tone. "Too many chemicals. Too much."

Manohar jumps to his feet before the Swede can lay a hand on the hulking Scotsman's dinner and gently takes him by the arm.

"Too many this side. Not even. Not even," the Swedish chess player tells Manohar.

"Night and day," declares Manohar quickly with a smile.

"Ahhh, yes. Night and day," A beaming smile breaks out on the Swede's face. "Yes, yes. Night and day."

"Would you like to sit with us?" Manohar tries to steer him away.

At the same time, two men and a woman descend the stairs from the mezzanine in a hurry. One of the men is dressed in smart casual clothes and sports a trim, mature figure. He bursts out: "What are you doing making a scene like this? There are friggin' media upstairs, you idiot."

"Not even. Not even."

The other two move either side to intervene on Manohar, and take the Swede's arms, relieving him of the troubled soul.

"Thank you for your help. I am his manager. We will take it from here," the manager advises Manohar. The woman produces a syringe and jabs it into the Swedish chess player's arm.

Manohar is horrified and exclaims, "Oh no, no."

But it is too late. The sedative kicks in and within seconds, the Swede is compliant and dreamy like, as a big smile appears on his face again. As they lead him away, he looks back over his shoulder at

Manohar and sings, "Night and day … hee-hee."

CHAPTER 7

"**A**LL THE UPGRADED rooms are fully occupied, I'm afraid. Of course, all the sponsors have standard booking, so they always are." She is dispassionate, forty, and the only admin worker at the office. She had arrived to find Helen waiting outside and standing behind her as she opened the doors. She doesn't seem in the mood to start work yet.

"Here is an application for a change of rooms. Some athletes don't stick around for the Closing Ceremony. A room may become available after day five or six."

"Five or six? But that is when our event starts," Helen appeals, but there is no reply. "Okay. I also need admission to the Media Centre."

The admin worker passes another form for Helen to fill out.

Helen skips through the form and stops at a page. "Passes are only issued through sponsors? We have no sponsor." She feels her anger rising and tells herself to stay calm.

The admin worker looks bored now and says nothing. Helen walks out with the forms still in her hand. This is going to be a problem. Billy needs press coverage. It is imperative to Wongii. It is her job to get it and the Opening Ceremony is only two days away. She needs to think and keeps walking. Her previous spurt of anger evaporates. Stumped, she wanders aimlessly.

*

After days of travelling and hour upon hour sitting in a confined position aboard a plane, Manohar now insists that the first priority is to clean out any toxin build-up in the muscles. Once breakfast is finished, the day begins with an extensive stretching session out on the fields, with Aaron leading the way. They start early but are certainly not alone. Athletes are out for morning jogs, and cyclists make the most of the early hours and vacant streets to get some distance practice in.

By the time Manohar is showing the way in a fifty-minute yoga session, athletes are buzzing by them, and the practice fields around them are a hive of activity. Footwork is an important aspect of many decathlon events—discus, shot put, and javelin, especially. And so, Aaron follows yoga with a series of spring steps from one leg to the other, skipping side to side, and crossover steps that are imperative for javelin. Some fruit and a fifteen-minute break follow.

Although they have decided that any hard training will be for later in the day, when Aaron notices short track lanes are available, with starting blocks in place, he thinks it best to take advantage of it. Out of the block, sprint starts last about twenty minutes until they are moved along by the Tanzanian squad who have the lanes booked.

"We will do a light run, Manohar. Four or five k's." Aaron looks across with raised eyebrows. "It will give us a chance to check things out …"

"Stretch your legs again afterwards, Billy," says Manohar. "I will prepare a meal. See you back at the apartment." The two take off immediately, and he is left with sweaty towels and the bag.

They set off across the field, down to the sands of the bay, and back up to the other side of the stadium. Only two kilometres in, they agree they cannot run past the Swim Centre without a look inside.

They decide a detour and quick walk through will not hurt and pass through the door panting.

Coaches pace up and down the pool as swimmers glide through the water and entourages skip from pool to pool. Billy notices a swimmer in the seating receiving an injection into his hand. Aaron points out the South Korean from the food machine at the cafeteria exiting the pool; the size of his hands is on full display spreading across the tiles. When he stands, they see his body is rippled, tight with muscle.

"Who would've thought Mickey Mouse was so ripped?" Aaron queries half joking, half in envy.

"It's all the coal he shovelled as a child labourer on the Mississippi, back in the day," mocks Billy.

As they wander through the complex, two female swimmers walk towards them fresh from the pool, their shoulders as wide as Billy's. But they walk oddly and lift their knees too high, as if in a comical march. It draws the attention of both Billy and Aaron to what is underneath the knees. Flipper-like feet … elongated beyond any semblance of comfortable walking; they have fattened, sausage-like toes hanging off. *More results of gigantism*, Aaron surmises.

By the time Billy and Aaron realise those are real feet impeding the swimmers' walk, they are ashamed of themselves for staring, and look away. When a chance arises, Aaron raises an eyebrow at Billy, and they pick up the pace.

The exit is blocked by the entry of the Russian female swim squad, and as twenty of the Chinese female squad are also leaving, they are forced to wait in line. There is no 'gigantism' amongst the squads, but it is apparent that their bodies are the products of long-term steroid abuse. Daunting, over muscled, and powerful-looking females surround the boys; some are so big that they look down on Billy. The two friends are too scared to stare now, and they become 'shy boys'. They look at their own feet, and they look at each other's feet, to avoid eye-contact.

Finally, they escape the crowd on the other side of the doorway, and immediately, they break into a run to get away from their own embarrassment and such a freaking environment.

They run at quite a clip for a jog across the hockey fields, around a residential block, and back towards the stadium. The day's humidity has started, and Billy can feel the difference between jogging in Wongii and Cuba. Aaron takes another detour and veers towards the Ice Arena.

Cool air strikes them on opening the door, which they both appreciate. Croatian skaters are collecting their gear and leaving and so are blocking the first aisle and any clear view of the ice rink. The Danish squad limbers up in the second aisle, preparing to take to the ice next. As Aaron and Billy don't want to get in anyone's way, they venture down the third aisle for a closer look.

Out on the ice and to music, a Cuban performer is in a figure skating spin. One hand holds a red sash that twirls and orbits her like a fiery Saturn ring. Leaving her spin, she skates in a wide arc across the rink with the sash trailing behind. Gaining a little speed, she tacks back and goes into a sliding cartwheel, from one foot to her hands, and back to her feet, all the while keeping the sash up off the ice. *She has ice skates on her hands!* Billy is amazed. She rolls seamlessly into another cartwheel and drifts along. It is mesmerising.

"Wow. The Olympics can have their ribbon twirling, synchronised, floor gymnastic ball-shit. Mash them together on ice is where it's at." Billy is captivated.

"Is that the sound of your traditional values cracking?"

Arcing again across the ice to gather speed, the skater goddess leaps into a double rotation and allows the sash to wrap around her body, shortening its length. She skates on, picking up more speed. In a classic ballerina move, she raises one leg behind, arches her back far enough to hook an ice skate-gloved hand behind it, and stretches the leg above her head into the splits, gliding forward on one skate.

Billy's mouth drops open as he realises that she has not just hooked her stretched leg, she has looped the sash around it. And when she falls out of the position, she falls into a handstand and begins to spin. Upside down, legs still wide apart in the split position, she spins with the red sash curving in an arc. She drops to one leg and one hand on the ice, unwraps the sash from the leg above, and stands to two feet on the ice, spinning to a stop. It appears that the sash is still dry.

Two men clap from the sides. "*Muy bien. Muy bien*," her coach calls out. As the Danish squad takes to the ice, she skates towards an exit and bursts into an enthusiastic wave to Billy and Aaron, like old friends would, surprised to find each other here. A big smile lights up her face, zeroing in on them. Though they are hesitant, at first, they still reward her with a little wave back.

All around the two men, things are buzzing. The Finns are lacing up or stretching out in one group and the Canadians are arriving in another, but Billy notices that the ice skater is now sitting alone, as the only member of the Cuban Skating Squad. Her trainer and coach are in deep conversation on the sideline.

She fumbles through a bag and manages to produce a water bottle between her ice skate-gloved hands. Unopened, and unable to take her skates/gloves off herself to open it, she looks to her coach and gives him a wave for help. But he is too busy to see her and continues talking to the trainer. She puts the bottle down on the seat alongside. Billy sees an opportunity and goes to her rescue.

He walks down the steps towards the front, and is only three seats away, when she raises a hand high and slammed the point of the skate down on the seat … water sprays everywhere. Billy hesitates, watching her clumsily lift the punctured water bottle to her lips and start slurping from its side. That's when she sees Billy standing awkwardly and she peeks around the water bottle to gaze at him.

"Ah," he swallows, "I was going to see if you needed help with that."

She stops slurping, puts the bottle down, and offers her hand to Billy. He wipes the excess water away and sits on the wet seat. She tilts her head at this. He begins unlacing her glove.

"You spin like a ball in water out there. It's amazing. I bet it's a lot of fun. I mean, lots of training, of course … but—" He finds himself babbling. "English?"

"Soy Cubana. No Ingles," she announces with pride and yanks her hand free from the skate. Her hand is wrapped and taped like a boxer's in a glove, but the strapping goes from the fingertips all the way past the wrist, to give extra support. She offers to shake hands, "Allisante Pascal de Cuba," she introduces herself.

"Billy Uke, Australia."

They shake hands and Billy begins to unlace the second skate, but her coach starts yelling instructions to Allisante in Spanish and indicating to Billy to get out of the way.

"Time to go," yells Aaron, coming closer. Billy rises and retreats back up the steps.

"Australia is a long way, Billy Uke," Allisante calls after him.

"Ah, you speak English?" He backtracks.

"Si," she waves goodbye. "*Adios.*"

He returns to Aaron, who has a grin and raises an eyebrow at him.

"Did you see her? Out on the ice? Amazing," Billy exclaims.

"I saw the wave she gave you and the bandaged hands. Look around you. You saw those injections by the pool. She could be a Lobster Lady for all you know," he smirks and jogs away.

"She is not a lobster," Billy yells after him as he too, breaks into a jog.

*

Helen has considered the time it would take to apply and process an application to register Wongii as an official sponsor. *It won't be done by the Opening Ceremony*, she sighs.

The Opening Ceremony is a chance to mix and network not just with the media, but with the large company sponsors of clothing, footwear, drinks, and sporting equipment. It is an opportunity for Billy and an opportunity for Wongii. *How can I find a solution by tomorrow night?* She racks her brain all the way back to the room, where she finds Manohar alone with the training bag.

"How did it go?" He asks.

"I don't like our chances of a room change." She does not mention the Media Centre or her concerns with sponsors.

"I think Aaron would be content in a tent," Manohar comforts her. Helen looks about for the boys. "They are exploring," he advises.

"What a wonderful idea. I need time to think. Let's take a look ourselves, shall we?"

They set out and walked past soccer practice, with little interest, to the Gymnastics Centre, which offers a greater variety. They enter to a hive of activity: men flipping over the horizontal bars and around the pommel horse; women spinning from one uneven bar to the next; and loud music beating for those on the floor practising their routine.

A banner strung overhead reads: *Genie Cosmetic Repression— Don't let your Genetics be Generic.*

Pixie-like contortionists bend too far on the balance beam under neath it. Way too far even for a yoga instructor like Manohar to tolerate; he thinks it unnatural. Miniature gymnasts, resembling pre-pubescent girls, flip across the floor. Others giggle as they stretch out or wipe down with Genie Cosmetics towels. Helen raises an eyebrow at him and gives a tricky grin. He squirms and feels he shouldn't be there.

It becomes apparent that the whole pharmaceutical strategy makes perfect sense to the cosmetic industry: create another Nadia Comaneci— the 1976 Olympic legend who scored a perfect 10 at the tender age of fourteen. But make a Nadia Comaneci that was Nadia Comaneci longer than Nadia was Nadia Comaneci and everyone will want to be a Nadia Comaneci. Nadias everywhere.

A couple rehearse their Acrobatic Gymnastics Mixed pairs on the next floor. Every movement is in time to the music … every lift, every twirl, and every spin. It is beautiful to watch. Helen and Manohar stop to admire the artistry.

The pair is made up of a male that is like an animated, ancient Greek statue, but only thirty-two-years old and African American. His partner is twenty, Caucasian, and tiny. She bounds across the floor and leaps into his arms in a well-rehearsed pose. He raises her high with one arm for all to see, spins around, lets out a blood-curdling scream, and drops her. Like a ninja, she tumbles safely to her feet and walks off. He hits the deck behind her and is immobile.

The music stops. In a flash, two medics in Titan uniforms run across the floor, pile the man on a stretcher, and remove him. Another man with a sponge and towel runs behind them and begins cleaning the mat. The medics rush the athlete from the arena, his manager in tow, and deposit him alongside Helen and Manohar. They leave immediately and return to their posts without looking back.

Manohar stares around in disbelief. The music starts again, and two new athletes take to the floor as if nothing has happened.

"Everything will be fine, Richard," his manager pats his shoulder once, pulls her phone out, and walks off as well.

Manohar looks at Helen and motions towards the medics back sitting in their chairs, but Helen does not think they should become involved. She points to his manager and beckons Manohar to leave with her.

"Damn, those painkillers are good stuff. I feel great," Richard suddenly blurts out. Slowly, he sits up, rubbing his eyes hard with one hand.

Manohar can't help but help. "Oh, no. Please lay down," he eases Richard back down.

"I can't even see straight. Damn good drugs. How's it looking down there?" Richard points to his legs while gazing at Helen.

"Oh, I'm not a doctor."

"But you can take a look. Things are too blurry for me."

Reluctantly, Helen takes a look. She recoils at the sight: his ankle is crooked and badly swollen. Quietly horrified, she lies, "Oh, I've seen worse."

"I worry about a fluid build-up," Richard continues in a dreamy, drug-fuelled voice. "I'm contracted to drink five litres of Beef Upjuice a day, and between you and me, it tastes like shit." He snorts. "I drink a gallon of water a day to wash the taste away. How's it looking down there?"

They can see it growing huge, inflating out the sides of an ice pack.

"Yeah, you do what you got to do. Sooner the better," he is quite jovial and well drugged by now and, rubbing his eye, he tries to sit up again.

Manohar gently pushes him back down once more, and Richard lets out an ironic chuckle. "I only started on the drugs because I couldn't get over an injury. Ha. How's it look?"

The toes are gruesome, bloated, and blotched red on the sides from swelling. They are four times the normal size of a toe, and Helen can't see some of their toenails. She is repulsed but still murmurs, "Uh … peachy?"

"Ah good. I really worry about the fluid. But fuck, I feel good," he smiles, relieved.

Helen turns on Richard's manager like a huntress. The manager has her back to Richard and is still on the phone. Helen strides across and circles her.

"No more African American athletes, please. They are a dime a dozen in sport, and the US is already saturated with drugs. Can we get a Chinese or an Indian this time? It's all about the numbers. Yes, the doctor is on his way? Okay. Talk later." Helen thinks she must be in her early thirties, and she is dressed in designer clothes.

"That man's ankle could be broken," Helen spits out, her voice shaking.

"Richard's? Oh, I'm not a medic but …" the manager screws her face up in an overplayed grimace, "Urgh," she shivers.

"Where are your priorities?" Helen snaps.

The manager looks at her, startled. She takes her earpiece out. "He's not in any pain. But he is in three team events!" She states defensively. She can see Helen's distress and touches her arm gently.

"Team responsibility, and responsibility to sponsors, right?" She says. "Look, I like Richard. I look after him. I've made a fortune for him out of Beef Upjuice. But the show must go on." She squeezes Helen's arm and swings away to make her way toward Richard.

Helen follows. There is absolutely no doubt that it is over for Richard. And it is undeniable that there is a responsibility to his team members. *The manager hasn't lied; she is right,* thinks Helen. *It is a show, and it must go on. But it could all end for you in an instant, with the breaking of your body.* The realities of professional sport come crashing down on her.

With a sense of doom, Helen looks across to a muscular woman as, regulating a puffing breath, she crucifies herself on the rings, doing the iron cross.

CHAPTER 8

THE MORNING BEGAN with stretching and yoga down at the beach before moving into the gym for strength training. Helen rose early to accompany them. She needs pictures and the morning proved glorious.

As Aaron partners Billy's core training on the gym floor with a medicine ball, Helen keeps clicking. She sends the images off to Janine. She also sends them to media outlets, inviting them to reply; these are sent to Australian newspapers and television stations, mostly. But as the day progresses, they are sent to British and European channels as well. Europeans recognise organic and non-GM foods. Helen hopes to push this as a human-interest story. She can only throw out the bait.

Billy works out on the resistance bands attached to a portion of the sidewall of the gymnasium between two racks of hand weights. He chuckles, loses his rhythm, and eases off. Coach Aaron turns to see what has distracted him and sees Allisante working out on the floor, just past one of the weight racks. She is twisted into a comical, bogus version of a particularly difficult yoga position.

"Is that supposed to be the Kapilasana position?" Aaron asks Billy. "Have you got your very own stalker?"

"It's not stalking if you want to be seen."

"We practised that position at sunrise … at the beach … I didn't see her there. Was she hiding in the sand?"

"So, first she was a lobster, and now you're calling her a stalker?"

"Hey, lobsters stalk their prey, brother. I'll give you a five-minute break, but then it's back to training."

Billy is delighted that the ice-skating goddess had taken the time to find him.

*

By late afternoon, at discus practice, Helen has become quietly concerned. Out on the field, Billy spins around under the watchful eye of Aaron, throwing into a large net that hangs loosely from a white frame that looks like oversized goal posts.

Other contestants practise from a different circle alongside, throwing into the same net. She has taken a lot more pictures, but the trouble is she does not know where else to send them. She has not heard back from anybody.

Bollards are being placed at the entrance to the stadium for tomorrow's Opening Ceremony. They are lined out for teams to enter in an orderly fashion and with each one placed, Helen feels a tick, then a tock. She finds herself fretting and picking at her shirt.

Marquees are being erected alongside the bollards and more of them over by the Media Centre. One by one, as the roofs are raised, a bright sponsor's name and logo appears: Yield; Gotta-Aid; Beef Upjuice (which comes in a variety of other flavours— Chicken Upjuice, Pork Upjuice, and Camel). All of these just kept reminding Helen that she is not part of the club.

*

Billy wakes with both excitement and trepidation about the Opening Ceremony. There will be hundreds of millions of people watching. And Wongii. For all his reluctance in coming to Guantanamo, he cannot ignore all the training and preparation he has done, let alone the work and money Wongii has put in to get him here. They have pinned their hopes on him. He doesn't want it all to be to no avail. His competitive spirit stirs as he lies in bed, looking at the ceiling.

I'm not part of the club. This is the first thing on Helen's mind as she wakes. It is early and she can hear the others getting ready to leave.

She springs out of bed and checks her emails: nothing. Sitting back down on her bed, Helen stares at her phone like it will make some sort of difference, willing it, mind over matter stuff. She does not know what else she can do.

The next thing she knows, the others are leaving. She ties her hair back, dresses in a hurry, and follows them, grabbing a banana for breakfast on the way.

Across the fields, hundreds of people are stretching in the early light and Manohar leads the way for Aaron and Billy. Helen stands off to one side with her back to them, staring at the marquees and their bright logos, as if trying to fit them together like a puzzle.

She is fifty-three and has no reputation here. Irrelevant. She has no power. She is not part of the club. It is not self-depreciation or a problem with self-esteem; she is working. She is analysing her position from their perspective, and they are the ones with the power. They have reputations, the brand names, and the money.

The action on the fields becomes more and more intense as athletes finish their morning stretches, and training began. Helen looks at Manohar and Billy, still holding a yoga pose. She looks back to the Beef Upjuice marquee across from the Media Centre and thinks of Richard and his manager.

An idea dawns on her. *The show must go on.* It is time to make herself relevant. "I'll catch up with you later," she lets her team know.

*

Helen is not in a hurry; she has time. She showers, makes coffee, and sits down to reconsider her idea and all its aspects. Questions will be asked, and she needs pre-prepared answers that sound logical. She dresses for business, in a pair of long, tailored beige slacks, a three-quarter length white shirt, and a pin-striped, tan jacket that matches her shoes. She sprays her hair to avoid any frizz from the humidity, and puts it up in a bun, checking none of her brown hair has fallen to her jacket or strayed. Two pieces of jewellery only. She gives herself the once over in the mirror and takes a deep breath.

Picking up one of her folders, she heads for the door, where she stops. Returning to the bathroom, she takes her contact lenses out and dons her glasses. *Better.*

When she arrives, The Media Centre is already lively and there is still the problem of security. She gives them both a wide berth and walks around the park behind the trees. The sponsor's marquees are also busy. There are entourages collecting matching commemorative clothing for the Opening Ceremony; trainers and coaches collecting passes for admittance to press areas; and pretty girls serving refreshments and morning coffees. The first lot of marquees belong to brand name shoe companies and sports apparel. She passes them for the Gotta-Aid stall.

"Helen Ellis, representing Billy Uke." She holds the folder upright and taps it on the table.

The Gotta-Aid executive is in his late thirties and tanned with an open-necked shirt displaying a gold necklace. He reminds her of a used car salesman. He starts checking his laptop and, screwing his face up, announces, "You are not with us."

"No. Not yet. But let's talk about that, shall we?"

He reads on, "HA! He is organic? Is this a joke?"

"Then you have nothing to lose. We do. But I could mitigate that risk by offering a public conversion of my guy to Gotta-Aid products on the second day of the Decathlon. Interested?" She pauses a moment before flattering, "A tiny promotional coup for a company your size, but coups are talked about."

"I'm listening."

"Your safety net? Even if people ridicule him for being a complete loser, he still reached for your product above any other, like say, Beef Upjuice."

"I like your way of thinking."

"Your bonus is he is genuinely talented and still young. Don't forget, he has made it here without any enhancement whatsoever.

Shall we discuss it tonight?"

"I suppose he has." He ponders for a moment. "I'll need to add your passport and room key to the pass." He opens a pack, and Helen passes him her passport and room key. He scans them and adds Helen's name to the list on his laptop. "Looking forward to speaking with you, Helen."

"As do I." They exchange pleasant smiles.

Walking off, Helen's 'pleasant smile' breaks into one of genuine glee. She passes the Beef Upjuice marquee and again thinks of Richard and his broken ankle. Clubs bought and sold athletes like equipment. She has seen it in many sports. But clubs were always on the lookout for new members. She is part of the club now.

CHAPTER 9

BILLY'S DEEP BLUE jacket is taut against his muscled arms and shows off his strapping figure. His trepidation has not passed, but he feels a thrilling pounding in his chest and a buzz of adventure as he walks to the stadium amongst the world's elite athletes. He notes Helen wearing earrings for the first time since he has known her. "Dressed to impress tonight, Helen," he says.

"Well, I am going to work." She is flattered by the compliment and clutches her necklace. Dressed in a long, formal evening dress with short, flutter sleeves, it is a light, breezy colour of purple orchid. It is elegant and simple with a high, wide material belt the same colour. It is an Opening Ceremony, a gala, and everybody will be trying to impress. "But thank you. Enjoy your night. Only days till you start work," she grins.

The Wongii Team stop before reaching the stadium. National teams are lining up behind flags outside the tunnel. "Manohar and I have to go through the east entrance. And I want a good seat," Aaron takes a few steps ahead.

"Well, good luck. Have fun. You've earned it." Helen holds up her pass, "I'm off to the Corporate Boxes," she finishes with a smile.

"Yes. Enjoy," Manohar waves and walks after Aaron.

Billy looks for the Australian flag. Finding it reminds him he is unwelcome, and for a second, he is intimidated. But it is his place to be. Head games, Aaron had called it. He pushes the feeling down and tightens his jaw. He lines up at the back of the Australian Team. Some of them turn around to see him, but they look away and ignore him.

They inch forward to the tunnel entrance under instruction from an official in a white coat. Crack, crack, crack. Athletes are already in line, and the teams from Vietnam, Yemen, and Zambia are waiting across the road in the field. They fall silent in anticipation. They look up. The boom of fireworks exploding above officially open the Titan Games and set the athletes off as one into a roar.

Reds, blues, yellows, and greens fall through the sky. It sends a thrill through Billy, and he finds himself clapping and cheering along with others. Coloured lasers flash through the smoke and into the night sky. Thousands of them begin blinking on and off, like they are in a scene from a *Star Trek* movie as laser bolts spear out from the stadium defending the Federation. It is an explosion in the sky of colour and smoke.

The stuttering lasers become a constant. They dance across the sky to form the word TITAN high above the stadium. The tunnel entrance is only steps away, and Billy has to lean back and arch his neck to see the words. Afghanistan is called.

Exhilarated, he tries looking over the shoulders of those in front as they shuffle along through the tunnel. He tries for a glimpse through the opening ahead, but it is just coloured smoke. Australia is called and the pounding in his heart jumps up a notch.

*

It is after midnight, in the bar at the Wongii Hotel. Power workers, farmers, artists, hipsters, and hippies have gathered. Barbeques are sizzling at farms where neighbours have come for a late-night visit, especially to watch the Opening.

On the screen, dancers in traditional clothing from all over the world are in unison doing the same step around a stage where a singer belts out an upbeat song. The hippy and alternative communes in Wongii dance along to it beneath a tarpaulin strung up between two buses. Lasers flash and national flags wave in the crowded stadium. It is so colourful. Opening Ceremony joints are lit, and bongs are hit.

At the Buckman household, Mary and Laddie are sitting forward in their seats. Mary keeps grabbing Laddie's hand with both of her own, then letting go. When the Australian side is called, she clutches hard at his hand. The team is led out by a female flag bearer and the camera closes in on her. The emblem on the top pocket of her shirt is of a musclebound, steroid-enhanced echidna, hanging over a paling fence. Claws and quills are razor sharp.

"Ooh. Angry echidna!" Laddie jumps back, "Rest in peace Boxing Kangaroo!"

"There's Billy," Mary cries excitedly.

*

"Wave. Wave as you enter, please," he can hear the official yelling. Billy can barely make him out through the blue smoke. Apart from the official and the occasional bang of fireworks, it is surprisingly quiet.

He pushes his way through the blue fog and into the stadium proper to no cheering whatsoever. There are no spectators. There are only coaches and trainers up front, and no seating beyond that. Certainly, no atmosphere. It is barren and stagnant.

Up high, a single wall of dark glass, close and overpowering, encircles the stadium housing the Corporate Boxes. Underneath, there is a green screen wrapping around the track four rows back from the fence. Automated cameras run overhead and along the fence rail. His smile dies, along with his excitement. It is all a massive letdown and his shoulders sag.

"Smile when you wave. Wave, wave please. Argentina, slow down," another official yells.

Reluctantly, Billy follows instructions and waves to … no one.

He feels stupid straight away. All he can do is keep walking and wave … and feel stupid, again. He thinks it so desolate, but there is also something else missing. Turning to the Austrian Team behind him, he asks, "Hey, not even music?"

"Ah, all spliced, my friend. Maybe Marc Anthony in Cuba, Shakira in Colombia, Willie Nelson elsewhere. Spliced like the crowd," he points ahead. "Split and splice them for a background to the soundtrack."

At the 100-metres finish line, real people sit twelve seats wide, twenty rows deep. Camera operators are set up before them under the guidance of a director. He spots Aaron in the second row, waving a Russian flag. Manohar is sitting alongside, waving an Iranian one.

As Billy marches closer, the Director yells, "Right. All change now!" He sounds like an English train conductor.

Nothing cheers him up more than the look of humiliation on his best friend's face, as Aaron puts down his Russian flag and raises a Canadian one. Manohar is now waving a flag from Bangladesh. *This is all such madness. Such bullshit! Why have seating if there is no paying public?* Billy's face breaks into a smile, and then he begins to chuckle. He makes sure that Aaron has to endure every step of his grin until he passes.

Cuba is announced.

Billy turns around and walks backwards, hoping to get a glimpse of Allisante. She is easy to spot. Alissante bounces out of formation and rushes towards the green screen, waving enthusiastically. She points to imaginary people in feigned surprise, putting her hands to her heart in appreciation, and then applauds them back. Billy starts laughing. An official struggles to get her back in line, as she blows kisses to her imaginary friends over his shoulder.

*

Shoes, sports equipment, clothing, health insurance. Hair products? *Billy does have a 'shock of hair'*, Helen muses. *And cosmetic companies would be here for marketing deodorants and the like. All viable options. Even a local Australian contract advertising their products would fetch a hundred thousand dollars towards a town battery.* This is the hook she is going for— greening the planet.

Helen is not naïve enough to believe any company would put climate change before shareholders, but there are carbon tax offsets and tax breaks on offer with money paid towards a battery and not the individual. Plus, she knows that advertising is not all about 'the flash and lights', but also about credibility. *And Billy will have plenty if he can hold his own, drug free, against this field, as Jack said he could. This is about a 'feel good' story,* she argued with herself, *and 'feel good' sells products*!

Before she can think about it anymore, Helen is handing over her Gotta-Aid pass to a security guard. He checks the invitation and waves her through. It is easy, and she is feeling quite clever as she climbs the stairs. Awaiting her at the top is a large ice sculpture of a beautiful swan unfolding its wings. They hover over a laurel made of bay leaves standing on a red silk pillow. The head wreath of victory to some, but Helen only wonders what Julius Caesar had to do with sport.

Left or right? The festivities run as far as she could see in both directions.

"Champagne?" She hears, as a waiter in black and white holds up a tray of bubbling flute glasses.

"No, thank you. Do you have a white wine? A chardonnay?"

"It is the '67 …" he ever-so politely encourages her.

"Oh, well, in that case. Better to say you have tried the 1967 champagne than to have not. Thank you." She takes a glass and heads left.

Exorbitant would have been an understatement, and even Helen, one who is experienced with promotional launches, is taken aback at the opulent exhibition that unfolds before her. Caviar, baked king salmon, lobster, king crab, exotic fruits, cheeses, and truffles. There is even an entire glazed wild boar taking up a table. Exquisite floral arrangements the likes of which she has never seen are everywhere. Strange and beautiful flowers.

A life-sized ice sculpture of two Grecian wrestlers grappling with each other stands to her left. It is perfect. Further along is a discus athlete carved in ice, followed by a runner, then a boxer. Sculptures of all the different sports run the length of the stadium corporate. Their smooth heads shine like gods in the overhead light.

There are glass display cabinets housing old worn-out shoes, cracked leather boxing gloves, and singlets from bygone days.

As she peers at them, Helen notices that some names and occasions are world famous, and everyone would have heard of them: Muhammad Ali's gloves; the four-minute mile and Bannister; Torvill and Dean's skates; the Berlin Games.

But there are fifty cabinets containing an assortment of soccer boots, bats, balls, golf clubs, shorts, rackets, jerseys, and 60-year-old jockstraps. And men. LOTS of men here. Maybe one in seven or eight were female … if you counted the wait staff.

There is no such ratio around the pig, though. Or the cabinets. All men.

Stay away from the cabinets!! She makes a mental note. *You don't know what is in them. It will become a 'mansplaining' festival of things you don't care about, and you will look stupid.* Squaring her shoulders, she reminds herself: *Stay on task, be available, and an opening shall present itself. Network.*

But in a spin that Torvill and Dean would be proud of, done in heels and not on ice, she spun a floorless about face as, just ahead of her, she spies the Gotta-Aid executive. Her action is a reflex, instinctual, and unfortunately for him, she notes that he is by a display cabinet … to make matters worse.

Helen has never intended to ask Billy to convert to Gotta-Aid. There is a pang of guilt for standing someone up, but this is business, not a date. She reminds herself she has a responsibility to her client first. Neither the Gotta-Aid executive nor herself need the embarrassment. "Retreat gracefully and no one will know," she mutters to herself.

"Helen. Welcome." A tall and impressive-looking man takes her by surprise, stepping into her path.

He is impeccable in his attire. Expensive, quality suits are everywhere, but he is standing in front of her, aloft of a single crease or ruffle from socialising. He carries no drink, and his air is one of comfort and control. *Is he the concierge? Did he see me ditch my Gotta-Aid entry ticket?* "Hello. I'm sorry, do—?"

"I am Mr Weeks, Managing Director of the Titan Games," he smoothly interrupts, bowing his head slightly, and keeping his hands together at his chest rather than offering one. "Welcome to our little gathering," he smiles. His teeth are perfect too.

"Pleased to meet you Mr Weeks."

"I wonder if we may have a word in a more private setting?"

"Lead the way," she chirps pleasantly, dishonestly, secretly concerned she is actually being escorted out of the building.

Her escort is too busy acknowledging guests with a quick bow, or charismatic smile, to talk to her along the way, or to give her any further indication of what is happening. He leads them through the gathering and then through a doorway; it is not to an exit, but to a plush reception office. Mr Weeks swings open the big door from here to his private office.

The lavish desk takes her eye first. It is simply beautiful, such intricate craftwork. She runs her hand along it, and Mr Weeks allows her time to absorb and admire. From his seat, Helen can see he looks across to two Picassos on the wall. A vase on a stand, under a glass case, stands between them. She thinks the vase is antique. *It could be Chinese,* she ponders. The white is still vibrant, and the blue is deep.

The wall to the right has a large flatscreen, and framed photographs of Mr Weeks shaking hands with the world's elites, and US Generals. Mixed among them are family pictures of what she thinks has to be his son through the years; sometimes in a wheelchair, sometimes standing, but on oxygen. The images showcase sporting heroes shaking the kid's hand, with Mr Weeks always in the background. In contrast, the entire wall left of the desk is bare and deep black … a perfect foil for migraines.

"No finishing line view as a job perk?" She asks.

At this, Mr Weeks presses a button by his liquor cabinet and the nano-glass clears to a perfect view of the athletes and proceedings below. He drops some ice into two glasses and grabs a decanter.

"Athletes come and go, Helen; it is the t-shirts that last. But with a little medicinal help from our sponsors … they can come and go again!" He starts to chuckle. "More money than the fucking resurrection of Christ."

"Uh huh," she sighs, unsettled.

"And we don't have to waste all that time and money on tedious drug testing facilities like the Olympics. 'Higher, Longer, Faster'—it is sooo 20th century. How high? How long? Can a man outrun a deer? This is what we market for the next generation. Which brings us to you."

"Me?"

"Very clever to bring someone drug-free here. And a stroke of genius in playing the indigenous card along with it!" A leering smile develops across his face as he holds both glasses tightly to his chest long enough for her to notice. He offers her a glass.

Taken aback at the insinuation, she hesitates before accepting the glass. "I don't know about playing any racial card. Billy has earned his place here."

"He's a nobody," Weeks declares flatly and sips at his scotch. "It is you who has earned a place here. I have been asked to facilitate the purchase of your contract with Mr Uke. And, I'm pleased to say, offer you a job."

Five minutes ago, she thought she was being escorted out. This offer is unexpected, to say the least. A genuine surprise. She scowls her doubt.

"You will find the terms very favourable," he entices.

Helen turns her back to Mr Weeks and looks down at Billy on the field below. She absorbs the sheer size of the competitors Billy is standing amongst and against.

"Surely you know he doesn't stand a chance?" Mr Weeks continues, his voice smooth and convincing. "He is a distraction. Nothing more. But you can still come out a winner. I understand you work from a home office?"

Stranger danger alert! It is only professional to check up on her, she considers, but she doesn't like it. And now she is reminded of her financial difficulties. "Oh, I couldn't possibly," her voice trembles.

"It would be exceedingly lucrative," he assures her.

She turns back around to speak directly to Mr Weeks, "Couldn't possibly … I have no contract with Billy. Can't help you. My contract is with the town of Wongii. I'm afraid you have been misinformed."

Mr Weeks is at a loss for words. *No contract?!* That does not make sense. The silence stretches out. Face to face it draws out longer and longer, until it becomes very uncomfortable for her, and it begins to take on a whole new meaning.

"Well, that does confound the matter somewhat," he announces, at last, his voice smooth once more. He steps past her to gaze out the window at the hype and the lights below. "I do hope we get to speak again."

Was that it? Did he really just dismiss me like that? She wants to speak up. She wants to scream, "Don't you turn your back on me, you misogynistic bastard. Have some common decency!" Instead, she quickly considers the repercussions of making waves with such a man. She cannot discard that drawn out, creepy silence.

"As do I." She's polite. The retreat to the door is humiliating.

CHAPTER 10

HELEN IS THE last one out of bed and Mr Weeks is the first thing on her mind. She needs a shower just at the thought of him.

The rest of the team has already left. So, she showers, makes a coffee, and sits down to dwell on her encounter with him before stopping herself. "It's defeatist!" She exclaims out loud. "It will do no good!"

She knows that her time can be better spent. More ideas are needed for media coverage.

Helen leaves the apartment soon after, to catch up with the others. She locates them on the Long Jump training track. More pictures will still come in handy for social media and so she begins snapping.

Billy and Aaron are on the track talking, but there is a girl sitting in the lotus position alongside the sandbox eating a bowl of rice and beans. When Billy runs down the track and jumps, she put the bowl down, applauds him, and then returns to her meal.

"He has an admirer," Manohar declares with a grin.

The thought perks her up. Helen positions herself to take some pictures and notices she is not the only one admiring. The Lithuanian athlete and trainer also watch on.

After Aaron has called it enough with the Long Jump practice, introductions are made, and Allisante has to depart for her own training. Thereafter, the Wongii Team has an hour's break and a light meal and moves on to the gymnasium.

Seeing the attention Billy gets from the Italian coach and athlete in the gym could be put down to coincidence, but when Helen sees the English and Iranian coaches together in discussion watching Billy, her confidence in him lifts. It was the Iranian and English coaches together, after all … Helen is intrigued.

Half an hour later, the same occurs with the Belgian and Chinese trainers. *If Billy isn't a threat to the athletes, he is a threat to their products. Jack could be right*, Helen muses.

It made it all the more imperative for her to get some mainstream media coverage.

*

They find a spot away from the well-lit dock where people walk and paddle in the shallow water at its beginning. There is a clear sky, the stars are out, and the moon illuminates the white sand along the beach.

It has been a solid day of training for them both, so Billy is surprised that Allisante still has such a spring in her step. If he were to use one word to describe her, it would be effervescent. They sit down in the sand to enjoy the cooler evening breeze and share a large apple, passing it back and forth.

"Oh, it is beautiful where I live too, but my town is broke."

"Ahh, we have to repair EVERYTHING in Cuba! Nothing new since before my mother was born. Uncle's car is kept together with coke cans." Her hands speak along with her. "They only let Socialists on this part of the island to play Capitalist Games. Phuh." She finishes peeved, and bites into the apple.

His first reaction is to explain himself better. Explain that in English, 'broke' also means poor. Instead, he stays quiet, and is rewarded with perspective.

"So," he continues, "we decided to try something new for Wongii—my hometown. We are trying to start a new industry centred around healthy food rather than coal. I'm here to promote that."

"I was the best gymnast in Cuba. I am National Champion four times," Allisante informs him. "Once I went to Spain. But they said 'my mente' broke like Uncle's car. How you say? Mind, *si*. My mind broke and they give me medication. Druggos." Her eyes express every emotion. Every up and down like she is onstage at a kids' pantomime. Billy is fascinated.

"My people say I'm crazy now. But I have no future in gymnastics, anyway. Soon I am twenty-five. Too old. But I *nunca* give up … Ah, never give up. I try a new sport, with new drugs. To be the best outside of Cuba. To win."

It is quite the tale. Billy cannot believe she is so point blank in just opening up like that about her state of mind. So candid that people called her crazy and mean it. But her tale explains how flexible she is out on the ice. "I guess I am lucky I have no pressure to win. I only have to stay up there and promote."

"Why do you only have to do that?" Allisante queries, her brow is furrowed in puzzlement.

"Don't get me wrong, I'm competitive. Competitive enough to raise questions. I just can't 'win' as such."

"How do you know this?"

"The drugs. I can't compete with them. Not really."

"Sooo … you train hard, to earn a place … to raise a question … that you do not want to answer?" Her brow and eyes have scrunched up even further, like she has seen a Rubik's Cube for the first time and is on the clock to sort it out. "Aaand make money for someone else? *Ah si*, normal!" She flips both hands in the air, dismissing his point of view, and looks out over the water.

Billy pauses for a time while he considers a reasonable rebuttal. "Well—" he begins, but Allisante shoves the apple in his mouth to prevent another word, and just like that, sweet, lovable, Allisante is gone.

"Worst pep talk EVER! Soy Cubana! Pfff!" Allisante's eyes are wide and accusing. "What do YOU want to know, Billy Uke? What will YOU try … for yourself? What will YOU be left with? Besides an apple. Huh?"

Her intensity throws him. Billy is still staring at her, dumbfounded, when the switch flips and sweet Allisante is back.

"But this is a really good apple, no? Any more?" She takes the apple from him and bites into it.

*

Helen is lying in bed with phone numbers, emails, follow-up calls, and schedules crowding her brain. She is glad Billy has stepped out to relax with Allisante. There is only one more day of training, and she assumes it will be a light one for him tomorrow.

She is struggling to relax though, and sleep is far off. Every time she puts the follow-up calls and ideas out of her mind, Mr Weeks sneaks back in. "Surely you know he doesn't stand a chance?" His mocking comment plays as a loop in her head.

Jack would strongly disagree, though, she reminds herself. She hopes Jack is right. *But is he?* She begins scrolling her phone for footage of the competition since the Opening Ceremony. She has been so profoundly busy trying to pry doors open and network with potential sponsors that she has not watched a single sporting event.

Scrolling past the weightlifters, Helen watches some swimming. She is amazed at the size and power of some and appalled at the gigantic Atlantis/Neanderthal feet of others. Gymnastics entertains for a while, but prepubescent girls are not a good comparison.

The tag headlines are all the same: *'The Amazing …', 'Unbelievable …', 'The Astonishing …'* until *'The Mismatch'* tagline catches her eye.

It is boxing. She detests boxing. But it is probably the truest comparison of Billy's predicament, and the most accurate Mr Weeks would apply—mismatched. She turns the sound up and listens to the host commentators of the Titan Games, Tim and Kym.

> TIM: *In and out with another sound combination, Rodriguez clearly outclasses his opponent, and the second round is an absolute thumping like the first.*

> KYM: *And another left. And another.*

A man with dark curly hair is ducking blows unsuccessfully, and he is running a lot. The other is Rodriguez: a moving mosaic of spider, skull, and crucifix tattoos, wailing upon his victim without mercy.

> TIM: *The Mexican is looking good tonight. We have the first round scored at 54 to 3. Rodriguez has got to be getting tired. He is spending as much time chasing the Palestinian around the ring as punching him.*

> KYM: *Twenty-nine, thirty. Glucose deprived, but cocaine invigorated. He will be sniffling for a week. But dare I say, a truly good boxer wouldn't require a snort after the very first round. Greed. His competition is rather bleak after all.*

> TIM: *I don't know how his competition is still standing.*

> KYM: *Yes, an absolute testament to his non-drowsy painkillers. Great drugs, Timmy. Great drugs. Not even a boxer! Al Saed tended olive trees before settlers gave him a career change. It was either Gaza or here. But his contract is not to win Tim, just to stay upright until the end. Great drugs. Great drugs.*

> TIM: *And a devastating right hook leaves Al Saed tangled in the ropes as the bell sounds to complete the second round.*

In the boxing ring, Rodriguez sits and is given a drink. He is sponged cool by his entourage, towelled dry, and tourniquetted off. A leg begins to bounce on the ball of his foot as a needle is injected into the other, and amphetamines are applied. Al Saed crumbles onto a stool alone in his corner and spits blood into a bucket. His Saudi Arabian trainer is sipping Turkish coffee outside the ring.

Al Saed splutters, "How ... is ... score?"

The trainer waves him quiet with a scowl and tosses a towel to him. He gives Al Saed a moment to clean himself up before removing his earpiece. "Ahhh, no score yet. El Massrae has had two shots at goal and Hussien one. The Belgians cannot hold out much longer. God willing, the second half will all be played in their half."

Helen can see Rodriguez doing a line off his glove in the background.

"Are you okay?" The Palestinian's trainer asks. There is no advice to give. He can't help him; Al Saed is a farmer, not a boxer. Accepting his lot, Al Saed simply nods his head. The bell rings again and Al Saed struggles to his feet.

"Do not worry, my friend. I will let you know if a goal is scored," his trainer calls out through the ropes, putting his earpiece back in.

Helen can't take any more and turns the phone off. Another round will give her nightmares. Mr Weeks's words lurk in the darkness: "Surely you know he doesn't have a chance?"

*

It is the day before the decathlon and there won't be any stressful training on the body today. No risk of some haphazard injury stifling the hopes of Billy and dreams of Wongii. Instead, they agree that Aaron will run through the motions and finer details of discus and shotput. Manohar has also allowed Billy to sleep in before starting the day with yoga. Allisante, and even Helen, have given it a whirl with them this morning.

Manohar takes a walk and wanders along the beach, waiting for the supply vessel to arrive. He cools his feet, strolling through the lapping waves of the bay while soaking in the sun. Across the shimmering waves under a blue sky, the *SS Stewie* is in the distance as it makes its way to Guantanamo. Sea gulls squawk and gather on the water, feeding on bait fish. Manohar isn't in a hurry as he turns around and heads back to the dock. He knows the ship will have to tie up, and there is an entire vessel to unload. He doesn't want to get in anybody's way. He reaches the dock when a small cafeteria refrigeration truck is almost full and the vessel's deck is almost cleared.

Cargo lines one side of the dock, leaving a passageway to walk.

"No, no," Manohar groans in a panic and steps away from the crate that is marked with the word, Wongii. *That moved far too easily!* He walks around it and checks the name on the box again. His concern deepens as he effortlessly pushes the crate along the deck with his foot.

"No!" He exclaims again and strides along the dock toward the vessel and its captain. Spying a flat bar sitting on top of some crates, he grabs it, runs back to the crate, and begins to pry it open. "No." Crack. "No, no." Two cracks later, the lid comes off an empty box.

"NOOO!"

He walks around in a tight circle with his fingers in his hair. *Maybe a different crate. A mix up?!*

Rushing back towards the *SS Stewie*, he scans the other crates and cargo along the way, desperate to find another crate marked Wongii. Every box, however, is marked: Titan Games.

He reaches the vessel and calls to the deckhands who are clearing the last of the deck. "Where is it? Where's the food?"

The crew point to the stacks of food crates that have been unloaded; they are ambivalent towards his state of panic.

"No! Our food!" He yells in exasperation. "Organic food. Delivered from Annotto Bay." They just shrug their shoulders and return to work.

"I want to see the captain!"

He double checks the stacks on his way back to the Wongii crate, praying for a miracle as he waits for the captain. He notices a receipt on the bottom of the Wongii box and retrieves it. His whole body is tight with anger as he waits.

*

There is no escaping the humidity. Even sitting under the shade of a tree, Helen's clothes still stick to her. After her attempt at yoga, she has showered and spent the morning in a futile effort to engage with the press. No matter how she pitches it, they all have interviews lined up with 'bigger names', or prior commitments to one of their sponsors who advertises with them. Chasing winners is the mantra. "If Billy Uke wins an event, things might change," they assure her.

Well duh! She muses.

It is even too hot for Helen to eat lunch. A piece of fruit was enough. Billy doesn't suffer from such a problem and scoffs his down. He is now lying on his back alongside Allisante, in the shade, leaving Aaron to eat lunch with Helen. Her phone rings. "Hi."

"It's gone. There is no food," Manohar says.

Helen pauses. She can hear the dismay in his voice. "Hold on, maybe the box has simply been misplaced? What did the crew say?"

"The box is empty. Well, except for the receipt. We still got charged. And the crew is no help. The captain just repeats: "Not responsible. Take it up with admin.""

Helen goes cold at his words. The shiver springs from the back of her neck and tingles to her forehead and heart: *Take it up with admin.*

She reaches over and places her hand in front of Aaron's mouth, preventing him from taking another bite. Into the phone, she behests, "Get back to the apartment, Manohar, as fast as you can."

*

"Shit. Shit!" Helen holds on to two overhead kitchen cupboards doors. The shelves are empty. The fridge has been cleaned out and their food box and suitcase are gone. "So, what do we have left, besides what's left of Aaron's lunch?"

Manohar comes from his room, shaking his head. "Herbal tea."

Billy has not said a word. With Allisante by his side, Helen thinks they look like a couple of lost puppies. Fretful. She knows that feeling; immobilised with not wanting to consider what comes next. This same feeling is currently threatening to overwhelm her, but she spits out: "I want answers. Someone must have seen something!"

Helen storms into the hallway, and stares down at the security desk. It is no use asking them. They are well aware of all the comings and goings, and likely, they admitted the perpetrators if not being the perpetrators themselves, as no one from the Wongii team has lost their swipe card key.

Instead, with narrowing eyes, she knocks on the door across the hall. With no answer, she knocks again.

A hulking figure opens the door. It is a disgruntled Māori. His face bears the traditional tā moko face tattoos. He stares down at her. *He has to be 1.98cm or 6 ft 5 inches*, Helen muses.

"Excuse me, I am from the room opposite. Did you see anyone enter our rooms today?"

She waits, but there is no response from the behemoth. "All our food has been taken," she continues.

From behind the door, a voice shrills, "Who the fuck takes someone's food?"

With that, the behemoth swings the door open for Helen to enter. He leans on the top of the door, looking across the hallway into the tiny Wongii room, staring at Billy, who is there with arms crossed. He remains there, staring, and keeps the door open until Billy accepts the invitation. Aaron, Manohar, and Allisante trot along behind him.

The Wongii Troupe slow as they enter, amazed at the size of the New Zealander apartment. It is ritzy with a sunken lounge downstairs and a huge wall TV. There are stairs … *Presumably to the bedrooms*, Helen thinks in awe. A large living area leads out to a balcony, and a full modern kitchen is off to the side with a dining table for six.

"Everything?" The man behind the door rumbles. Another Māori athlete; Billy recognises him as a man built for speed, as he appears to be about 185 cm, and is lean, agile, and well-muscled. *Probably late twenties*, Helen muses. He looks like he is about to burst out of his skin, as he taps the side of his leg, his eyes dart from one visitor to the next, and his one-word question is almost shouted.

"Everything," Helen sighs. "All our organic food from home, and the shipment from Cuba. Everything is gone."

"Organic? Did you say organic?" He queries.

"We are chemical free. No drugs."

"No drugs?" The man does not wait for an answer. He spins around to Billy and, in disbelief, he shrieks, "You don't take drugs? How can you not take drugs?"

Helen is determined not to be distracted; she wants to stay on task. "And because no one has lost a key, I really don't trust security anymore. I don't even trust the tap water now."

"Oh, come on. Eat the chocolate, enjoy a wine, see the sunrise … and just take some drugs, cuz." The man persists in his own private conversation with Billy. "You are here to compete, aren't you?"

"Shh," a third member of the apartment waves at the man to be quiet. Walking forward, he goes to shake Billy's hand. "You are decathlon, right? I'm Rob. This is Mikey. Sorry, he gets a little excited. And this is Vincent." Fair skin, curly hair, and mid-thirties, Rob is not a New Zealand athlete. He didn't really have a title and was there to keep Mikey out of trouble more than anything. And the simple fact that everyone else is too scared to room with Vincent makes Rob an excellent choice of roommates. He even has a calming effect on the behemoth.

Rob looks up at Vincent and raises an eyebrow. "Three days? No food or water?"

"I have some bottled water. I'll share with you," Mikey offers. Billy sighs with relief.

"Yeah, Mikey has a contract promoting his spring water from the South Island. So, you know it's clean," Rob assures him.

"I've told you before; it gives me power," Mikey explains to Rob like he is tired of explaining it. "It's my 'magic spring water' from tribal lands."

"You're on three uppers and two steroids. I roll joints to bring you back down."

"But it's the magic water that gives me my power," Mikey insists.

"You're an idiot."

They snigger together like the stoners they are, before Mikey points to six cases of bottled water on the kitchen floor beside the refrigerator. Vincent steps past everyone to the stack. He looked to Rob first and motions his head towards the staircase, silently indicating he will keep them upstairs in his room for safekeeping. He bends down for a case.

"Ahh, it looks like the big fellow has decided to watch over your water for you," states Rob.

But Vincent puts his hands under four of the six cases. Dismayed, Mikey jumps across to the kitchen, "Hey, hey, I said share. What are you doing, man? Can you even count?"

Vincent gives a look of thunder and steps forward to the challenge. Mikey backpedals quickly, and for a split second, everyone in the room feels his panic. Content with the result, Vincent calmly returns to the bottles, and lumbers off with all four cases.

"Ha. What happened to your 'power', Mikey?" Rob giggles.

"He doesn't say much, does he?" Helen whispers.

"Well, no one has spoken to him for six years back home. So, I guess he kind of gave up," Rob explains.

"Whoa? What did he do?" Billy blurts out and immediately regrets asking that about a man who is helping him. Especially while he is still present.

"Sports gambling addiction!" Bursts out Rob. "Vincent threw a match and got a lifetime ban. He keeps to himself mostly. Generally, he tries to make amends …"

"Generally!" Mikey squeals, before yelling up the staircase after Vincent, "But now you're stealing my magic, big man. You Northern Tribes are fucking savages."

"My God. Six years?" Manohar shook his head. "So how long will this public shaming go on?"

At the top of stairs, Vincent pauses, floating on hope, and listening in.

"Cuz, we're not Native American. We are Māori! And he gave the Rugby Cup to the Aussies. The fucking Aussies! His ghost walks alone," Mikey wails.

The weight of shame descends yet again on Vincent, crushing his hope. He lumbers off in silence with the water.

"But he's the best security you can get. You are welcome to hang out here if you like."

"Oh, thank you, Rob. Thank you, guys." The tone of Helen's voice changes to a battle mode. "Training is over."

Completely out of step, Allisante brings her fists to her chest and vibrates them like she has just won a prize. "Yesss." With a grin of triumph, she snuggles in under Billy's arm.

"Conserve all energy," Helen instructs Aaron. "Keep him well hydrated," she urges Manohar, rushing to the door. "And don't move till I get back!"

*

Helen tempers her frustration with manners. She is absolutely certain that Mr Weeks has his hands all over this. Yet here she is at the counter of the Administration Office. It doesn't help her frustration looking down at the twelve pages of forms that she has been given to fill out, all neatly arranged on a clipboard.

"I don't think you appreciate the urgency here. His race starts tomorrow morning," she adds tight-lipped.

"You've said that," replies the young and bored administration worker

She is not responsible. It is not her fault, Helen has to remind herself. *She is just doing her job, doing what she is told, and is probably on a temporary contract, anyway.*

Taking the clipboard and pen, Helen walks out of the Administration Building and across to a park bench under a tree. She knows this is a waste of time, but she considers it prudent to leave a paper trail. To leave some sort of evidence of foul play. The team is depending on her. Organising and securing the food is part of management's job. Her job. She is supposed to know what to do if something goes wrong. A feeling of inadequacy surges over her; she is suddenly conscious of how naïve she was to think Weeks would take no for an answer.

*

The initial panic has subsided, though worry remains. It is etched on everyone's face in the Wongii team. The New Zealanders are natural hosts and do their best to take the Wongii squad's minds off their troubles.

Mundane questions of getting to know one another have quickly fallen aside with Mikey and Rob's irreverent back and forth, along with Mikey's antics. Aaron, Manohar, and Rob settle in on one sunken lounge, while Mikey stands in front of the TV searching with the remote control. Allisante snuggles up to Billy on the other. Vincent sits behind them all on a chair, not quite joined in yet not quite alone.

Everyone is being so considerate to Billy, so consoling. He isn't comfortable with any of that and feels it is misplaced. It wasn't his idea to come here. In fact, he recalls thinking it was a silly idea from the start. Now, without food, it all seems surreal. *Farcical, really*, he muses. *In the end, food will be found, the panic will have been for nothing, and it will be all the more farcical. There are a thousand athletes here, and thousands of other people in their entourages. That's a lot of food and a lot of different diets.* He is confident that Helen will find a solution.

The attention from Allisante is a different matter altogether, though. This he is thoroughly enjoying. He had not counted on meeting an exotic, foreign, older woman. Though Allisante may laugh at, or take offence to being described that way, she is all that to a twenty-one-year-old male from Wongii, Australia. *She is not 'beautiful' in the classic sense of the word,* Billy considers. *Better than that … She is different.*

Allisante is fun. She wears her emotions like sparkle-filled, luminescent paint. It is captivating and makes his heart skip a beat. He felt it the moment he laid eyes on her.

"Ahh, here it is. This was only this morning," Mikey says.

"Oh, no, not again," Rob lights a joint.

On the big screen, an oversized Turkmenistan weightlifter walks out to the floor. He is excessively hairy from testosterone abuse and little tufts of dark hair hang over his white socks. He dips his hands in a dish of lifting chalk, and it beads like snow on his knuckles; he rubs them together, and the snow falls away. Moving to the centre of the stage, he stands behind a gigantic barbell no man should be able to lift.

"That's not right. He is huge." Manohar is aghast from the start.

"Wait for it," teases Mikey.

The athlete grips the bar and heaves the weight to his chest, squatting to meet it, as is normal and expected in the competition section titled Clean & Jerk. But his belly button pops out. Not a 'little outtie' kind of thing, but a penis sized protrusion jumps forth, poking his singlet out from his stomach. Manohar's gasp fills the room. The competitor's bulky thighs power him up to a standing position, and the 'outtie' protrudes further, wobbling about like a gruesome teepee made of jelly. Mikey immediately points it out to his guests, "Yeeaah."

"*Que?*" Allisante jumps forward, eyes wide like a dinner plate.

"God, what is that?" Billy forgets all about his troubles.

Manohar involuntarily empathises with the athlete and swings his head towards the kitchen.

The giant from Turkmenistan is in the zone and committed. He grunts, shifts his leg position, and embarks on the final jerk to raise the bar above his head. His singlet thrusts forward like there is a snake escaping his midriff. At the 90% mark, he drops the barbell and falls to the floor clutching his stomach, bellowing like a cow. "Urrrr," Aaron cries as he, Billy, and Allisante run away. Manohar heads for the balcony door for air.

"Yeah," Mikey roars, happy with the reaction. "Yeah!"

Rob sniggers into his joint as Vincent joins in with a deep, slow chuckle.

"Turn that off. I can't stand listening to him," Billy calls over his shoulder as the weightlifter 'mooes' on like someone has stolen his calf.

"Yeah," Mikey says, one last time, before Rob takes the remote control away from him.

Flicking off the earlier recording, the screen reverts to live streaming, and music fills the room. It is thumping bass electronic music, with a crazy, wonderful, jazz top end full of sounds only a machine could make. A chess board is on-screen with many of the pieces already fallen. Swaying back and forth holding his headphones, the DJ is about to make his move.

"It's Not Even," Aaron calls out in surprise. The New Zealanders look at him, confused. "Manohar. It's your friend, Not Even, from the cafeteria."

The chess/mixing event, commonly referred to as DJChess, is in progress. With only minutes between moves, the conventional stop clock has been replaced by a mixing desk and song. Competitors have to successfully mix the opponents' song out, and your song in, as you make a move on the board. It's about counting beats, keeping tabs on how many music bars, whilst deliberating strategic moves to stay ahead of your opponent on a chessboard. This has proven too much for most. Many hopeful DJs have attempted the sport but failed at the intricacies of chess. And urban legend has it that the best chess player in the world is now in a psychiatric ward banging against a wall trying to get a song out of his head.

Manohar rushes back into the room, still full of concern for the man's wellbeing. He thinks that the Swedish chess player looks well. He looks at ease, a far cry from his previous state. In fact, he appears to be enjoying himself, deftly turning dials with one hand while grooving to the sound, his head bopping from side to side. In his element, he raises his other hand and begins pumping it in the air to the beat.

One song begins to disappear as a new one takes its place. He drops his hand and moves the queen.

KYM: *That is checkmate! And with a lovely drop, Tim.*

TIM: *I don't know what that means.*

The chess player stands in triumph, still pumping his hand to the music. The screen flicks over to a Stockholm nightclub full of wasted Swedes for a moment and back. Manohar lets out a sigh of relief.

*

It has taken longer than she thought it would, but the forms have been filled, with the last page requiring a full statement, one that Helen took her time to give. Details mattered. Returning the paperwork to administration she is told, "You will be contacted." *I'm not going to hold my breath,* she almost snaps back.

It has been hours since she stood before the empty cupboards in the Wongii apartment, and all she has managed to do is register that there is a problem. Determined not to go back empty-handed, Helen pulls out her phone to give a closer inspection of Aaron's picture of the food ATMs. They are lined up together along a wall. *So, what is behind that wall?* She peers more intently at the screen and decides, *It's time to find out.*

The sky is darkening by the time Helen makes her way to the cafeteria; people are already coming and going from their evening meal. But it isn't the food ATMs she is looking for and she bypasses them to head to the back of the building and the loading dock.

Empty crates are piled outside a clear-sheeted opening at the top of dock steps. Luckily, there is no one around. Deploying all of her non-existent ninja skills, Helen sneaks in, not really having a plan. Prepared meal carts, ready to go, are to the right. "Those are of no use to Billy," she whispers, whilst glancing left and right and feeling a thrill of anticipation course through her body. She can see the silhouettes of workers preparing meals through another sheeted doorway straight ahead. She will have to be careful. To the left, stacked high, are unopened crates ... again no use. Further ahead though, in front of the crates, are boxes of fruit.

A cautious look around, and she takes a quick step, venturing to the fruit. The sheeted door swings open, and a worker enters. Helen ducks down in the aisle to hide. She can hear him singing to himself as he searches for what he needs.

Crouched, she watches him through the gaps between boxes and waits for him to return to the kitchen. She stands, still on her guard, and is delighted to find she is standing over a box of apples. Keeping one eye on the doorway, she lifts two, but twenty more flow out. Fumbling about, she struggles to put them back, but they all appear to be attached to one another.

In an alcove between the unopened crates, directly behind her, a Latino woman and a man are sitting on boxes enjoying their meal break. They smile to one another, amused and puzzled at the clumsy show taking place before them.

"Can I help you?" The man asks.

Jumping in surprise, Helen drops the apples she has managed to gather. *I've been busted,* she frets.

Flushed with embarrassment, she turns around to face him. He is lean, his skin deeply weathered and tanned from decades of working in the sun, but he is not yet grey. She then embarrasses herself further, "Oh, English? Sorry about your apples." She knows she sounds stupid.

"Well, I am from Texas. And those are grapes."

She is dumbfounded. She grabs a grape to take a closer look.

He stands, "What exactly is it you are after?"

"Food. Unprocessed natural food." Leaving her astonishment behind, she speaks with urgency, not wanting to waste this opportunity. "There must be vegetarian athletes?"

"Of course. These are their grapes."

"Organic, I mean. Anything not genetically modified, or sprayed, or ..."

"All modified, I'm afraid. Do not go into the meat section." He scowls a warning and shakes his head.

"Surely something? EVERYTHING can't be connected to drug companies."

He stares at her, appreciating that she is rattled about something. He can hear it in her breathless voice. "Everything is connected by contracts. Pharmaceuticals are but one thread." He tutors her yet still manages to sound soothing. "There is broadcasting, clothing, gambling, food, and …" he indicates to his co-worker and himself, "… low wage labour agencies. The military even bid for the medical files when it's over."

He sounds calm and worldly. Philosophical even. Worse still, he sounds right. She not only believes him, she understands him. And a sense of dread falls on her. Without the proper food, the team's efforts appear to be thwarted. She feels utterly deflated and begins picking at her shirt, tears threatening after such a long day.

"Sorry, but you're on the wrong side of the island," he continues. The man beckons her to accompany him down the aisle to see more fruit. "The things I've seen in the meat section …" he shudders.

*

Still waiting in the New Zealand apartment, Manohar sits forward on the sofa. He is confused and trying his best to understand Mikey's point of view. "Wait. You only take party drugs, but you don't touch cocaine? Isn't coke the biggest party drug of all?"

"Party drug my arse. Five men in a circle, with one telling a story about himself? The only thing the other four are thinking is, *Oh, I got a story about me. I got a story about me.* NO ONE IS LISTENING!"

The door opens and Helen ambles in. When the room sees she is carrying a brown paper bag, they rise to their feet. She has saved the day.

"Hey, hey! Helen to the rescue," Aaron declares with enthusiasm.

Helen makes her way to the dining table without responding and waits while they gathered about it in anticipation of what is in the bag. Aaron pulls a chair out for Billy and Allisante, and sits down alongside Mikey.

Helen pulls a banana from the bag, places it on the table, and steps back. It stands upright in an ungodly manner, splitting halfway to form two distinct legs. They are two fat legs that enable it to stand proud to be a banana. Billy leans in for a closer inspection, his eyes squinting in disbelief at what he is seeing. Mikey lays his hands on the table and his head falls on top of them, studying the legs.

"It looks like a headless dinosaur," announces Aaron.

"Fruit does not have legs!" Billy growls and sits back in the chair.

An uneasy silence follows and lingers as the banana commands all of their attention. Bananas should not stand. It is one of the fundamental rules of the universe, like gravity, or water freezing at subzero temperatures; it shouldn't turn to milk. Lost, the people at the table gaze up to Helen for guidance, like she will have an answer or idea.

"Ahh … Smooth pineapples look like rugby balls …" she shrugs her newfound truth. It is the only other thing she can enlighten them with.

The thought of NO FOOD begins to sink in for everybody. Billy is left wrong footed, and a sinking feeling begins to take over. He was certain that Helen would find some food. Edible food. *How can I possibly compete without food?* He thinks.

In the silence that ensues, trepidation is beginning to be replaced by hopelessness. Not just for Billy, but for the Wongii squad and Wongii.

Mikey lifts his eyes to meet Vincent's. "Think they taste like chicken?"

Vincent chuckles deeply and in a flash, he snatches the banana from the table and runs off like a child, away from Mikey.

CHAPTER 11

"YEAH, SORRY ABOUT that." Aaron only half apologises as he drops his plate in the sink. Breakfast consisted of two eggs, four slices of toast, tomato, and a little bacon and beans, gratefully cooked by their New Zealand neighbours. Aaron is not going to go hungry on principle alone. He is not competing … so genetically modified food will do for him!

"At least Manohar had the decency to eat next door." Billy has had to endure the aroma and each mouthful.

He tossed and turned in his bed for hours before dozing off. He is accustomed to eating a vast amount of food as a twenty-one-year-old, and as a young man in training, even more so. Last night's half sandwich, leftover from Aaron, is not going to cut it. But it is not just that his stomach growled in protest at the smallness of the sandwich, it was that worry had taken his sleep.

Everyone back home in Wongii has invested so much time and effort in him, especially Janine and his parents. They are pinning their hopes for solar panels and a town battery on him. And so far, he has just gone along with the ride. Lying in bed, he feels helpless and foolish for being here.

Inevitably, during the long, drawn-out preamble to slumber, his thoughts had moved from Wongii to himself, and hard questions arose. Deeply personal questions of worth and abilities. Specifically, Allisante's questions.

"What will I be left with?" He states out loud. *The answer to that is easy,* he muses. *Absolutely nothing if I do not begin the Decathlon. Not a memory of it, or even a regret of what I could have done better if there is no start.*

"What do you want to know? What will you try?"

Hearing those two questions, as he speaks out loud, and picking them to pieces is another matter. It takes time, and it is uncomfortable to sink into, but it ends up going back to the same questions he has always asked himself: *Am I as good as the other athletes? Do I deserve to be here? Can I keep up with them?*

Billy knows that he needs answers, and suddenly, he jumps out of bed, reinvigorated.

*

No one paid much attention to the Cuban Press. In fact, much of the Western media ridiculed them for not telling 'the truth'. Instead, they argued amongst themselves about which one of their outlets was responsible for the 'fake news' in their own countries. It was the kind of patriotic masturbation that left everyone blind: hiding beneath the covers of a flag, banging away to yourself, until all you saw was your own fantasy.

The Cuban Press, all six of them, are gathered at the end of the street to the residential complex, where the fields begin. It is a sunny morning; the light is good, and they look at one another, unsure if they are conducting an interview with Allisante or receiving a lecture from her.

"*No queremos hambre aquí.* Ahh no, no." Brow furrowed, she wags her finger down the barrel of the camera. "*Esso es Cuba! Ladrones de comida. Bah.*" she rails and throws the back of her hand towards the press.

The literal translation, she later tells Billy is: [We don't want hunger here. Ahh no, no. This is Cuba! Thieves of food. Bah.]

"*Todos la isla es nuestra. El es nuestro huésped!*" She glares, in defiance, at the camera. [All the island is ours. He is our guest!]

Glancing past the press, her anger suddenly disappears and her demeanour changes to a smiley face as she gives a wave. "Oh, *Buenos Dias*, Helen."

Across the road, Helen marches towards the Titan CEO's office, her jaw set tight. The Cuban Press swing their cameras around to capture her. She doesn't wave back or reply. Her stride is long, and she is focused and on a mission. Allisante changes her wave to a fist and raises it high above her head, "*Viva Cuba!*" She cries.

Helen can see them in her peripheral vision, though she doesn't turn her head. She doesn't slow or skip a beat, but her hands are clenched into fists by her side. She punches them both up and forward in a double uppercut and holds them there.

Allisante's smile falls away. "*No como esso. Whoosh, enojada.*" [Not like this. Whoa, angry.]

*

Arriving at Mr Weeks's reception office, Helen waves away the receptionist as soon as she opens her mouth. "We can dispense with the pleasantries," she snaps out.

Instead, Helen speaks directly to the man in the polished suit who is standing behind her. In his mid-thirties, and impeccably groomed like Mr Weeks, she presumes him to be his personal assistant.

"I want to see Mr Weeks. I do not have time for the run-around."

"We will contact him now. Please take a seat." He motions his hand towards the guest lounge. "And you are …?"

"I don't want a seat. I want Weeks."

The man stops the secretary from using the reception phone and taps on Mr Week's door himself before entering. Helen paces the floor of the office with an eye on the large screen that is on the wall. It shows a distance shot of a track line up. The ticker tape running along the bottom reads: *First Decathlon Event – 100 m.*

The commentators appear on screen, and Helen can put faces to the commentary of the boxing match that had so appalled her. Tim, the conservative, polite, sixty-three-year-old anchor-man, is the ultimate professional to let into your living room. He begins the coverage:

> TIM: *Good morning, everyone, welcome to today's coverage. As always, we welcome the insight of the only dual Olympian and Titan Gold Medallist, as both male and female. Good morning to you, Kym.*

Kym is vivacious. Still chiselled fit at forty-seven years old, with short cropped, curly, bleached blonde hair, the earrings are fabulous. Bright, confident colours, and fashionably dressed, he comes across as dignified and stately. Helen is reminded of an androgynous John McEnroe, and she recognises Kym as a polarising character from years ago: hormone levels swinging so wildly and frantic that there is no hope of keeping anyone happy, inside or outside of sport.

> KYM: *And a very good morning to you, Tim. Quite the line-up today, and with those magnificent legs, the 'Grasshopper' stands the clear favourite.*

The 'Grasshopper' appears on screen, bouncing about and limbering up. Helen can see where the nickname comes from. He is easily the tallest in the lineup. His thighs are not just grossly enlarged, they are elongated and seem to swallow the knee. They rise, insectoid like, to the outskirts of his hip. But for all the talk of prowess and his legs, when he stands still and puts them together, Helen thinks they look like childbearing hips running down to the calf muscle. They are nothing like that of an insect. She shudders at the unreality of it all.

The screen splits to show close ups of other athletes in the line-up. Billy is one of them. *His first race and he is half-starved!* Helen's heart starts to gallop.

TIM: *Absolutely. Then, a rather unusual entrant. Claiming to be drug free and organic, Billy Uke from Wongii, Australia, takes on the most comprehensive body of athletes and scientists ever assembled. With ... lentils!*

KYM: *Luck with that. Can't help but question the wisdom when he is yet to compete in the Nationals. Ambitions mixed up with abilities, I'm afraid.*

As the runners take their positions, Helen stops pacing. *I should be down there, not here!* A tumble of emotions race through her.

The contestants crouch into the starting blocks and begin to set their feet. Helen looks over to Mr Week's closed door. His secretary lowers her head. *What is taking so long?*

"On your mark." She looks back at the screen. "Get set!" ...
BANG!

Heads down, they spring in unison. As they lift their heads and stick their chests out, arms began to swing, and the pace increases. They are a single, even line for the first forty metres or so, and then the line began to break when top speeds are reached. Helen catches her breath in her throat; her heart is pounding.

There isn't much in it, but the Kenyan, the Grasshopper, and the Algerian take the lead from the rest of the field. The three press on, but the thighs of the Grasshopper own the final strides. As the Kenyan and Algerian's dramatic burst of energy become exhausted, and they decelerate ever so slightly, the Grasshopper's thighs power on. It was all over in nine seconds flat for a 100 m race!

A bunch of athletes then cross the finish line at once. Helen cannot tell where Billy finishes, but the scoreboard board placements show Billy placing fourth in a field of eight. A smile creases Helen's face. It is a very respectable result.

The media rushes past Billy to the winner. Dozens of microphones are shoved in the space where the Grasshopper is gasping for air.

"How do you feel after winning today?"

"Is this the result you expected?" And so the 'exclusives' begin.

"Mr Weeks will see you now," Helen hears above the babbling reporters.

*

Mr Weeks is sitting behind his desk like a lord, or a judge, waiting for the next case. It is so obviously a choreographed display of power for Helen as she enters the room.

He stands and walks around the desk to greet her. "Helen, I have just heard the awful news. Let me assure you, we are searching every vessel, retracing every step of the way—"

"Don't give me that crap." She walks straight by him to the far end of the desk. "Someone was in our room."

He hesitates, and she can see he is not used to being spoken to like that. He clasps his hands together and brings them to his chest, sermon-like, in a pulpit, and takes a step towards her. "And Security is looking into that also," he adds. "We have a large team at our disposal. The very best money can buy."

Helen turns from him, taking steps of her own in a body-language ballet or a dance off, and makes him wait for her reply.

"Well, that may well be the problem," she says, circling his desk. "This is your responsibility. They were your security officers that let this happen. And as a CEO, the responsibility ultimately falls to you."

Mr Weeks tugs on his cufflinks and shirt sleeves. "My responsibility as a CEO is to the Titan Games. To see to the transportation and accommodation. To provide food and cater for all religions and cultures that attend." He raises his chin piously high. "Not YOUR chosen ethics, Helen."

"Ethics? Oh, please! It is a *freak* show out there." She takes another step, passing the corner of the desk to his side.

It is a step too far for him. She has invaded his private space.

"How judgmental of you!" He feigns indignation. "Not very

empathetic to the choices people make with their own bodies, are you? Especially for a woman," he notes darkly.

They lock eyes and there is a pause.

"Ohh, don't do that! Don't do that!"

But the gloves are off. He isn't going to play games with her anymore. He strides back behind his desk and pulls a drawer open. He doesn't try to hide the prescription pills or cocaine in it. He reaches in and draws out five identical, pre-prepared contracts, and slams them down on the desk.

"Billy Uke flies out to Jamaica on one of our jets today … as a duty of care, of course. And you all sign a Non-Disclosure Agreement." He reaches into a second drawer and holds up five fat envelopes of money. "Put this towards your town battery, if you like."

"Or alternatively," Helen sneers, "I could scream interference to the press."

A malevolent smile creeps across Mr Weeks' face, as he queries in a creepy, soft tone, "And how has the press been treating you so far, my dear?"

Her cheeks flush. *It is him! He is the reason why the media is too busy for Billy and Wongii. He is their 'prior engagement'.*

He drops the money on top of the contracts and waits for her to pick it up. "Doesn't have a chance," he reminds her.

Helen is crushed. A choking feeling begins in her chest and trembles its way down to her fingertips. Without some sort of media coverage, it is all dead ends. *This man is despicable*, she fumes and then adds, *and he scares me.*

Mr Weeks hovers over the cash like a dark shadow. She wants to get away … anywhere will do. She backs away from him and walks towards the door, hoping her legs will not give her wounds away or reveal her fear.

As she reaches the door, he calls after her, "Do be a professional and inform Billy Boy of the compensation on offer. His clock is ticking."

It isn't that far down to the track, but it takes a while as Helen urges her legs to keep working. *I have left with my dignity*, she thinks, *but nothing else.* And dignity is not enough … it certainly isn't going to feed Billy sufficiently for him to compete. She has responsibilities to see him fed, and the food has been taken right out from under her nose.

Once she has put some distance between herself and Mr Weeks' office, and is out of sight from prying eyes, Helen decides that she has to sit down. She is shaking; her whole body is one big shaking jelly. *Misogynistic. Asshole. Corrupt!* She finds herself almost picking a hole through her blouse and has to fold her arms. With pursed lips, she berates herself. *Stop being offended by this creep and be professional. Think.*

Helen rattles her brain, searching for a solution. *Who can we turn to?* But there is no regress that she can think of. Not here. Here, there is no one to tell. This is still Guantanamo Bay, and no laws apply. As far as she can tell, the only semblance of law is contractual, and the laws of Mr Weeks.

As for the media blackout, that's another problem beyond her control. The Wongii Team desperately require the press coverage. Wongii and its products rely on it. But with Gotta-Aid and Beef Upjuice spending millions on advertising with the media companies— dependable regular money— Wongii and Billy are not going to get a look-in. She now knew they were onboard with Weeks.

"Separate yourself from the problem and be coldly professional," she tells herself out loud. "Act with your clients' best interests at heart and not your dignity. Be like a defence lawyer."

These thoughts make her feel dirty. She doesn't like it, but she is loath to come up empty-handed for her client.

*

The second event is the Long Jump, and the team are beginning to wonder what has happened to Helen. The day is getting hotter, and perspiration is beginning to show on athletes and non-athletes alike.

Billy gave it everything he had in the 100m. He is pleased with his efforts, and he is happy with the result. *A good start,* he muses. *Better than I expected.* But the lack of food is now a discomfort; hunger pains are starting to gnaw at him. His belly has been growling ever since.

On the straight of the track, between the track proper and the fence, he looks across to the Long Jump lane and sandbox. Billy can feel the heat coming off the track as he walks out to take his place amongst the other contenders. He waits for his name to be called and watches his competition as he waits. There are some athletes built more for power than speed, and their attempts are in the same league as his own best jump the previous year. But there are others that are both inspirational and imposing. Beyond his hopes, in fact.

With a sigh, Billy walks into position when his name is called. He stares down the track to the sandbox. He is utterly focused as he bends forward, hangs in a little, and then leans back for one last look at the box. He prances forward off his mark in long hopping steps, all the while looking at his feet. As he lifts his head, his speed picks up. Arms swinging from side to side, he hits top speed. Hitting the line, he springs from one foot, thrusts his arms and legs forward and straight, all the while keeping his gluteus maximus up. He soars and then hits the sand. Right out of the box, on his first jump, Billy breaks his Personal Best by two centimetres.

Aaron and Manohar jump to their feet, applauding.

KYM: *Good effort, but he is no medal contender in this field of 95, Tim.*

The Grasshopper is next, and he lives up to his reputation.

TIM: *And the Grasshopper easily betters the Olympic record by 4 cm on his first attempt. What an amazing comeback after four years retired, Kym.*

KYM: *Four years, two marriages, and three paternity cases. Cocaine and Viagra had a lot to do with it, Tim.*

On his second attempt, Billy sprints strongly and springs joyfully into the air well. But suddenly, he lets his guard down and his bottom falls back to touch the sand and leave an imprint. A white flash shimmers across his eyesight in an unwelcome surprise, and he has to take his time stepping out of the sandbox. His body begins to quiver: it is objecting to more energy being expelled, especially after the 100 m sprint, without more nourishment being put in. He doesn't say anything to Aaron or Manohar, but he needs to squat down for a minute until his visuals return to normal.

Billy waits for his final attempt and thinks about his mistake. He then dismisses it. *It was just a sloppy finish,* he excuses. *I will do better.* Rocking back and forth on the track, and taking deep breaths, he prepares himself for his last jump. He pictures his success: His legs raised, arms reaching, hips up and forward. He visualises his landing, and he takes off in a sprint to chase it.

Billy hits the sand to equal his first jump. He wishes he could have done better, but it is still the best jump of his life. *I'll take that.*

TIM: *Well, he is no threat to the Grasshopper or the Kenyan, and like you said, Kym, he is no medal contender.*

*

Waiting for the third event, Billy towels himself dry, closes his eyes and tried to sit still. His stomach bays at him for attention.

Conserve all movement, he tells himself. But he cannot stop his brain from ticking over and his impatience growing for the next event to begin. If he had his way, there would be no waiting between events; he knows that he is just getting weaker. And that begins to irritate him. The more hungry he becomes, the more irritable he becomes. He is using up energy just holding it back. *Try to relax. Meditate.*

"How are you holding up?" Helen's voice pulls him out of his trance-like state.

"I'm okay."

"I can hear his stomach from over here," announces Aaron.

"Well, it didn't go as planned. He didn't offer food, he offered money. A very healthy bribe for all of us to sign a privacy contract. A Non-Disclosure Agreement. But Billy would have to leave today."

"That's not publicity," retorts Billy.

"There has been NO publicity so far. And after that meeting, I don't expect any media coverage now."

There is a long, drawn-out pause. Helen gives them time to process the news.

"You simply can't continue like this, Billy. It is unsustainable. Over a three-day period, it becomes dangerous." She glances across at Manohar on the word dangerous. "Without options, it may prove to be the most expedient course of action."

"Expedient?" Billy raises an eyebrow.

"That is not why I came," Manohar says.

"Oh, I know that. It's not what any of us planned for." She points up to the stadium and sighs. "I have been sitting on the steps up there for an hour, racking my brain, trying to find a way out of this mess. And I'm not going to lie to you—it's bad. We still have no food, no publicity, and no prospect of publicity. As much as it pains me to say this, it is my professional opinion we may have to cut our losses."

"How big was the bribe?" Aaron asks. "Grandad would say, 'Run now and ask for twice as much later!'"

"No chance! These are the Big Boys, and Weeks would happily let people starve. There won't be a 'later' without food or media. Without media coverage, this all becomes pointless."

Aaron hangs his head, and the team goes quiet, once again. Manohar takes a seat and rubs his face. But after a while, Billy starts to fidget in his chair.

"Pointless for you."

Helen can feel his challenge. *The poor kid must be horribly disappointed.* Helen chooses her words carefully. "Pointless for my client:

the town of Wongii," she corrects him. "I don't want anyone coming away empty-handed. That is my responsibility."

Billy holds her eyes for a time, but the thought of Wongii 'coming up empty-handed' forces him to concede. It is a bitter pill to swallow. He slumps back in his chair and withdraws from the world.

*

Mr Weeks opens a drawer to his seventeenth century desk and ruffles through some prescription bottles. He pours a glass of water and ambles across to the window. Looking down, he searches for the Wongii Team; he smirks when he locates them all sitting with their heads bowed. It is what he expected. It is not the bowed heads, or a feeling of victory over Helen, that pleases him. It is the predictability of it all that has made him happy. It shows he is in control.

Weeks swallows two pills and sips some water. Glancing back at the team, he focuses on a streak in the glass pane. He pulls out a silk handkerchief and begins rubbing it away.

CHAPTER 12

HIGH JUMP IS the third event, and it has already begun. Officials with wet collars fan themselves cool in the heat. Helen wipes the sweat from her brow and neck. But Billy brushes Manohar away when water is offered.

One by one, athletes' names are called, but trackside, the Wongii Team sits in an uneasy silence.

Billy is stewing. Every name that is called just builds more pressure. Allisante's simple question of, "What do you want to know?" has robbed him of sleep, and now, it is likely to go unanswered.

Can I keep up? The injustice of it all fuels his anger. It is not an emotion that he is used to dealing with in Wongii. He squirms in his seat and hunger feeds the fire that is thrumming inside of him. *They are no better than me!*

A Kenyan athlete is called. He too, has humongous thighs and abnormally long legs like the Chilean. The man clears the bar with such ease that he lands on one foot and walks away. History's biggest step goes unnoticed.

TIM: *And the Kenyan equals the Olympic record. Could he prove a match for the Grasshopper? Only time will tell.*

KIM: *A perfect example of targeted medication, Tim.*

"The drugs make them better." Billy hears this as if it is a voice inside of his head as injustice and anger bubble away. "They are 'injury prone' or making comebacks like the Grasshopper."

The ache in his belly warps his earlier admiration for the man. It bubbles away and boils down until the only emotion that is left is defiance. "They are old. I am not," he whispers determinedly through gritted teeth. "I have youth on my side … and youth gives the courage to make a fool of yourself," he growls then smiles wryly. Bouncing up, Billy pushes his hunger down, and starts stretching.

"Are you sure you want to do that?" Helen asks.

He ignores her and continues stretching.

"Have you thought of Wongii?" She reminds him.

He has. He is no longer concerned about Wongii. He turns to Aaron, "When the day is done, we hit the beach. See what she has to offer."

Aaron nods agreement, and Manohar grabs the sports bag to join them. They rush off to the inner track together, leaving Helen behind.

She purses her lips and watches them leave. She rubs her forehead, trying to erase this morning's stress and the thought of Mr Weeks. Before she knows it, she is checking her phone hoping for a lifeline. There is a message from the bank with the word urgent in capital letters. "Ah, shit!"

*

Irritated like never before and fuelled by resentment, Billy runs on the spot, manic in his warming up. He thrusts high in leg raises and bounces from one foot to the other. He burns energy with abandon.

There is no later, there is only now. Only this.

Billy stretches hard; he is hungry and impatient for the man from Belarus to begin. Billy's name has been called, and the Belarussian is the only one before him.

The man is big and heavy for a decathlon athlete, with a barrel chest and forearms like Popeye the Sailor. Billy remembers that he ran surprisingly strong in the 100 m, but discus, javelin, and shot put were his specialties. Not High Jump.

The Belarussian sets off with an air of confidence and authority; he makes a sweeping run towards the bar. He swings his anvil-like arms high, to get the momentum to hurl his herculean upper frame over the high-bar. But his approach is like a drunken lemur on the catwalk. With no poise whatsoever, he tosses himself into the Forsby Flop and crashes through the bar.

Billy sets the bar at a level he is confident of for a first jump. He has three attempts to prove himself, and points are taken only from the highest achievement. He readies himself, and trots in like he is catching the same bus he catches every day. With ease and grace, he pops over the bar, untroubled.

The commentators don't even acknowledge him. The Games screen coverage splits to show a wide shot of Billy sprawled on the mat from a distance on one side, and a close-up of the Kenyan athlete's face on the other.

TIM: *I mean, just how high could the world record be after the Kenyan's next two attempts?*

*

It seems like such a long wait between jumps. Manohar runs to the ice machines provided to teams under the stadium corporate boxes and returns with a fresh ice pack. He wraps it in a hand towel, pours water over it and slings it around the back of Billy's neck. Billy notices that for some strange reason, his stomach has stopped growling. He wants to get straight to business while it is behaving.

As soon as the official calls his name, he strides over to stand off to the side of the Belarussian, waiting for him to finish. Determined to validate himself, Billy sets the bar one centimetre higher than his Personal Best. It is a long way short of the Olympic record and will not surpass the Australian one. But it will be his best yet … his best ever.

Billy pictures it for the briefest of moments. *I can do this.* He is certain of that. The lead into the jump is fluid, and he leaps with perfect timing. He clears the bar. Rolling straight to his feet, he looks back at Aaron with a proud smile. *I did it!*

The global televised coverage, though, only shows a split screen comparison of Kenyan and Grasshopper legs. Particular attention is being paid to the thighs. It measures their length, their estimated proportion per kilo, and an 'expert' is commenting on the muscle to meat ratios (once the bone has been taken out, of course). It is a brief coverage, but it seemed important for the viewer to be informed about this.

*

In the Wongii Bar, pressure is showing. Hippies who hate the drug companies run outside for a joint between jumps to calm their nerves. They suck ferociously on them like they are the last remaining pocket of air in a sinking car. They pass the joints along to their friends and hold their breath until they are returned.

Morning Light almost knocks his own lights out when he runs into the door, rushing back inside.

*

Billy is ecstatic with the result. Euphoric. *I knew I could do it! It is a new Personal Best!*

Billy jokes with Aaron on his return: "Outdo that, brother!"

But that was easily ten minutes ago!? The euphoria has not subsided like it should have. Not completely. A smidge remains and everything else is slower, calmer. "Oh no, I'm lightheaded," he sighs.

Trying not to draw attention to himself, Billy sinks lower to the ground and places the ice pack under his arm. He drinks more water. He stays down there, at ground level, stretching out his hand to steady himself. *Urgh, this is astroturf,* he broods. *I don't like the feel of it.*

Okay ... think strategy, he chides himself. *One jump left. If I can* clear two more centimetres, my overall points jump more, with an unofficial new Australian record to boot. But that's risky. It might be smarter to think about the longer game of the Decathlon under my particular circumstances. Every little bit helps, though. I have a better chance of clearing just one more centimetre.

Doubt creeps in. It is the enemy of top athletes. 'Ifs', 'chance', 'buts', and 'mights', have replaced *'I can do this'*. Suddenly, Billy is no longer confident that he can. Suddenly he is thinking about: *Under my circumstances.*

When the time comes, Billy determinedly gets up and sets the bar at 1 cm above his newfound Personal Best. His approach is flawless, as is his timing, but his leap is lethargic; his body has nothing left to give. There is not enough gusto in his legs, and he clips the bar, and it falls with him.

The white light returns, and it steals the colour of the world away from him. The mat feels like a soft mattress. He doesn't want to get off.

TIM: *And after a Personal Best, the Australian fails.*

KYM: *His PB simply does not cut it here, I'm afraid, Tim.*

"He is running out of steam," declares Manohar.
"Ah, come on. He got a Personal Best," Aaron replies.

*

On the side of a mountain, where the road ends, the pueblo's poverty is assured. There is no industry or job prospects, only what they can grow and undertaking repairs of what they had. It is green as far as the eye can see, but it is all jungle below. Dilapidated motor bikes, one with a funky homemade sidecar, are all gathered at the end of the street with passengers, riders, and backpacks.

An old lady in the street throws up her hands in the air at the biker atop a heavy, 1970s three-wheeled motorbike. "Allisante de Pascal es Loca! *Ella tiene problemas de salud mental.*" [Allisante Pascal is mad! She has mental health issues.]

"*Si abuela, pero esso no la hace equivicada. Esso es Cuba!*" [Yes, grandmother, but that does not make her wrong. This is Cuba!]

To the younger generation, the ones that are Billy's age, the biker is no longer middle-aged Jose—the one who sleeps on the veranda after two beers—but The Man who Cut the Wire! It is a title that they have awarded to him, and they rally around him.

"Ah no. *Todos Locos*," a second grandmother waves him away.

But Jose remembers hunger and his small meals as a child. He remembers his father drinking sugar water instead of dinner and cursing the US embargo, preventing fertiliser for crops. Worm farms and community gardens have not fully solved the problem of food security, but it is now organic, and there is more. And the younger generation is now holding back the cut fencing wire to Guantanamo Bay, waiting for their leader.

Jose rides through the hole in the fence and bashes a way through the scrub on his trike, leaving a trail for others to follow. They weave their way across the mountain until they find the long disused road leading down the foothills to Guantanamo.

*

It is early afternoon, and the sun's heat is intense. It is an actual presence; a closeness that is draining everyone's strength.

An official on the track faints, his hat not offering enough protection. The fourth event, the 400-metre, is underway. Contestants are divided into heats and the Wongii Team waits for Billy's turn.

Helen occupies her time running through various scenarios in her head. She has a bad feeling about this. It is not today that she is worried about; she has lost control of that. Her concern is how bad things can get tomorrow. If Billy is ruined with no energy, and flops along the way, she has no doubt that Mr Weeks will set the media dogs upon him. Wongii and its products will become a laughingstock and a joke. Billy is playing with fire.

So, I was unsuccessful. Push it aside. I have a new PB, he thinks. *Concentrate on what is next, not what has passed.*

As far as he is concerned, Billy has validated his efforts with a Personal Best; it is a good thing and the first step in answering his questions has begun. It only makes him more determined. His stomach has even given up on growling and constantly reminding him of his hunger; it is quiet. However, he feels listless during the wait for his next event, though. He doesn't want to talk. Instead, he meditates.

Drawing lane six, this places him on the outer track and well onto the first turn. He takes to the field, gives his calf muscles one last stretch, and bounces about getting the blood to flow in limbering up. *400 metres,* he argues with himself. *One lap, with everything I have, and it will all be over with. 45 seconds or so. I can do this; I can do this.*

The eight competitors take their positions. With feet on the blocks, silence falls across the stadium as everyone waits for the starter's call.

"On your marks." They freeze into position. "Set." They raise up to their fingertips, and the gun fires.

Billy springs out strong, accelerating to top speed in the first fifty metres. He finds his rhythm coming out of the bend and into the first straight. He just needs to hold on and sustain it. His legs pound down the straight until they feel like they do not belong to him. They are on automatic now.

In the second turn, the rhythm changes. It drags and slows and no matter how hard his mind cries out to his legs to pick up the tempo; they are deaf to him. Without sustenance, there is simply no fuel left, and he begins to peter out. *No. No.*

It is gruelling on his body, and a savage blow to his confidence when the French and the Latvian on the outer lanes begin to pass him. Reaching the 300-metre mark at the home stretch, Billy can see the entire field, every lane, all are ahead of him. He pushes and pushes, willing his legs, but they have stopped listening. He fades away badly.

Billy finishes a distant last; he is 6.5 seconds behind the winner. A full two seconds behind second last; a stumpy-legged little Samoan, who is only there because he can just about throw a shot put out of the stadium.

Crossing the finish line, Billy winds down to a stop, and rolls to the ground, exhausted. Knees up, he is gulping and gasping for more air. He lies on his back with one arm over his head, and one splayed out on the track. The track is unbearably hot on his back; it is baking hot after seven hours in the sun. He had no choice but to roll over and pull himself up to one knee. Billy does not appear healthy: His face is pasty; he is the only runner not on his feet, and an official looks twice at him, before warning, "If you're going to be sick, move to the sideline."

TIM: *A dreadful display by Australia. Billy Uke will drop a long way in the field after that!*

KYM: *Organic food is one thing, but at least take some amphetamines to make it interesting.*

Dragging himself to his feet, Billy places his hands on his hips and sucks hard, still trying to draw in air. His head swoons. The colours around him swirl, and people appear to be moving in slow motion. *Whoo, dizzy!*

He tries to walk, but it is an embarrassing mashed-up, funky version of *Do the Hokie Pokie*. His left foot is shaking all about; but it does not know whether it wants to go in or out. It is like stepping in space. A marionette on the strings of an inebriated puppet master.

Up in his aerial office, Mr Weeks sweeps the envelopes of money back into the drawer of his desk and fixes himself an afternoon gin and tonic.

*

Two farmers and a power worker sitting at the bar of The Wongii Hotel put their beers down and turn around to look accusingly at Jack. He grunts back at them in defiance and takes a big swig of his beer.

All the tables of the bar are full; they are occupied by a group of hippies or hipsters, power workers or farmers, drunks and drug addicts. Murmurs filled with shock and worry spread from one table to the next. Soon, the hippies are looking to the farmers, hipsters to drunks, and power workers to the alternative crowd. Smokers stand and leave the room, needing a cigarette; hippies pull out emergency joints and head to the carpark, and those on 'happy-happy' pills feel their smiles seep away.

The Uke family, Janine and Dale, sit alongside Jack; they are all engrossed in what is happening on the big screen. No one can hide their concern watching Billy stumble about like that. Janine reaches for her phone.

*

Whilst other runners are walking out to the track for the next race, or limbering up in their lanes, Aaron and Manohar escort a depleted Billy from it. In the few seats provided, Helen stands and watches on. She is worried about his health now, and in a panic about tomorrow. A panic about Mr Weeks, a panic about Wongii, and a panic about being homeless at her age. She picks at her shirt like she is digging a splinter out. *Can this day possibly get any worse?*

As Helen's phone buzzes, her chest tightens; she knows exactly who it will be. She looks at it and sees that her fears are right. It is Janine.

"Oh, dear," she sighs, letting it ring while she takes a deep breath and steadies herself.

"Is he okay?" She hears the voice of Mary Uke.

"What's happened?" Asks Janine.

"Manohar is with him now," Helen states in the best calming voice she can muster. She looks across to see Billy pulling strange faces and then he crumbles to the ground between Aaron and Manohar. She can faintly hear his groans of pain as he cramps up. "Ah!" she swallows. "I'll put you on hold and take you to him." She tries to sound cheery and unconcerned.

She arrives to find Manohar standing over Billy, stretching his leg back, and attempting to ease his pain. Billy is moaning and still pulling strange faces.

"These cramps will continue. He can't go on." Manohar has seen enough.

"Ah, come on. It's Shot Put next. There is no running involved," Aaron interrupts.

"In this heat, he will pass out." Manohar is steadfast.

"Manohar is right. I'm not comfortable with any of this. Billy, we have to take the money while it is still on offer. There's still two more days to go! We have no option."

"I'm not taking money," Billy stutters in pain.

"Put it towards the town's battery! YOU HAVE NO FOOD!" She sounds like an aunty scolding a teenager's stupid act. "Look at you. You can't even stand. And now I have your mother on the phone."

"Don't mention the food," he says, his face straight and serious now.

"Oh, come on. I can't lie." She scowls back at him.

"I don't want my mum worrying."

She opens her palms and implores him, but Billy is adamant, "Please."

Helen hesitates, torn between business and family business, but she squats down alongside him reluctantly. It is his mother, after all. Helen puts the phone on speaker.

"I just need a rest, Mum. It's hot here."

"You need more than a rest," Helen retorts.

"Are you okay?" Mary asks.

"I'll be fine." Billy assures her.

"But I won't be," says Helen.

"Can you go on, son?"

"Yeah. I can do this."

"I'm sorry," Helen cuts in. "Valiant effort, but it's over, I'm afraid."

"You work for us, Helen," Janine reminds her. It did not come across as mean, or authoritative. It is more gentle and confident …

even airy. She can hear the good vibe intended. "Time to have a little faith, my friend. We trust Billy." Guru-like. But to Helen, it is naïve-hippie-speak up against Weeks. She purses her lips and clenches her jaw to make certain she stays quiet.

CHAPTER 13

PEOPLE ALL AROUND stand up and begin to yell. A commotion breaks out in the middle of the field and the track officials run towards it.

Some officials wave flags, stepping into the lanes, and the following 400-metre race comes to an abrupt halt just after it starts. Coaches and trainers run on to the track, screaming objections to the officials. Tempers are high and arms are being thrown about as runners come to a stop: they are milling about confused.

Aaron and Manohar, still with Billy's foot in his hand, try to make out what the fuss is all about. "What is it? What's happening?" Billy gets up on his elbows.

Security comes running from the tunnels. The Grasshopper's coach throws his hat to the ground and boots it away as all hell breaks loose. The guards meet in the middle of the field. Their hands are on their radios, receiving orders. A few jog towards the commotion, while others step across to calm trainers and coaches. But two remain, and one points out the Wongii Team to the other. The two make a beeline for them in a double step march. Utter confusion occupies the rest of the track.

"What do these two clowns want?" Aaron pipes up.

"Have to go!" Helen hangs up on Janine. She doesn't know what the trouble is about, but it is coming straight at her. Thumbs dance on her phone, checking the TV coverage to find out before they arrive.

TIM: *And I can confirm we have an official down, Kym. An official down with what I am told is a … papaya.*

KYM: *There seems to be some pandemonium coming from the Hockey Fields involving avocados as well, Tim. And a flying guava has something to do with it.*

"Avocados?" Aaron is sceptical.

Helen is as confused as the rest of her squad. She ponders for a moment, thinking out loud, "Avocados … Cuban avocados," she surmises.

She looks down at Billy, still sprawled out. "The organic hub of the Caribbean …" She recalls the claim of the Jamaican Customs Officer. Then she remembers Allisante's press conference. "Allisante! Aaron, it's Allisante. It's organic. Go, go, go."

Aaron's puzzled look changes to a mischievous jeer before he bolts off running.

TIM: *Our Eye in the Skye reports unauthorised movement on the mountainside above Guantanamo Bay, Kym.*

Aaron sprints towards the nearest exit; to the right of the approaching guards. They continue on course towards the rest of the Wongii Squad, but one guard is on his radio immediately, relaying a message to the others: "His coach is on the run. He is heading for the tunnel."

Aaron makes it to the entrance and pounds through the tunnel. More guards begin to pull a barricade across to close the exit and head him off, but he doesn't slow down at all. Without hesitation, he leaps and clears the barrier in an easy hurdle.

"He is not a coach. He is not a coach!" The guard cries into his radio, correcting his superior.

Aaron is fast. Very fast. And this time, he is running for more than beer money or gambling chicanery amongst friends. This time, he is on his own and running for one of them. The best of them, as far as he is concerned. His best friend. He sprints away and heads onto the Hockey Fields.

*

Jill wears a hat; it is a wide-brimmed hat to protect her fair skin. Her rosy cheeks shine under it, feeling the heat. It is an old, well-worn hat, and she light heartedly describes it as, "Frumpy, like myself." Jill is a freelance photojournalist of some note, and as she squats down on one knee, she is snapping pictures of a guard appearing to pick fruit salad from a hockey coach. *Somewhat unusual!* She grins to herself. The coach is lying dazed and wet on the ground with juice in his ear. Another guard is rushing around collecting scraps of smashed fruit that have ended up on the field; he is throwing them into a plastic bag.

When the guard's attention suddenly turns to the running figure (Aaron), it piques her interest. She stands up and, like any good journalist after a story, she holds her hat down and runs after him.

Aaron zig zags left and right, looking both up to the sky, and down on the ground, searching for food as he makes his way haphazardly across the field. He looks like an escaped chicken running from a fox. She chooses to run straight, as fast as she can, still wondering what the hell is going on …

Puffing away and falling further behind, Jill is glad to see an end in sight. Up ahead, a fence blocks any further chase as cyclists are lapping Guantanamo Bay in the 220-kilometre Men's Individual Road Race competition on the other side. The fence is tall and encompasses a long stretch along this part of the complex. The overhead walkways are as wide as a street, but they are well spaced apart.

TIM: *So, this could be some form of political protest involving Cuba, Kym?*

KYM: *Or avocados. Avocados and water theft seem to go hand in hand, Tim.*

*

Heads turn upwards as they hear a helicopter approach. A young man with binoculars is keeping a lookout on the old roads that begin down at the Guantanamo Bay complex. Dirt flies up as a motorbike with a funky sidecar pulls up on the towline, but the wheels are still slipping.

"*Mas pez. Mas pez,*" Jose calls out. [More weight.]

Straps are secured to tree trunks; they are made from inner tubes and surgical rubber, and they are being stretched to breaking point as makeshift slingshots. The woman in the sidecar stands to help another passenger aboard the backseat of the bike. She leans her weight over to the driver. The wheels finally bite into the ground and the bike lurches forward.

TIM: *An international incident is unfolding before our eyes. Not in a hundred years of occupying Guantanamo have the Cubans breached the fence, Kym.*

A young woman with a machete steps in and swings hard, slashing the towline. *Phwhack!* It makes a sound they have not heard before. Food flies off far into the distance and cheers and applause follow.

TIM: *Not a shot fired. Not even through the Cuban Missile Crisis.*

"Gringos!" Shouts the lookout. Humvees have started to make their way up the road.

"*Vamanos. Vamanos!*" Jose yells to everyone. But he has not quite finished. Tied up for one last shot, he pulls the slingshot tight. Passengers grab empty backpacks and jump aboard with the other riders, but they do not leave. "*Vete!*" He yells. [Go!]

But they wait. They will not leave without The Man who Cut the wire. He punches the heavy three-wheeler ahead for all it is worth.

The towline is slashed, papaya is launched, and he is set free. The escape is easy with such a head start, and through terrain that a wide four-wheel drive cannot traverse.

The whole adventure is exhilarating. Their hearts pound and they scream with primal excitement through the jungle on the way back home. Everyone has a tale to tell. The tales will be recalled and enjoyed by all for many a day, though Jose often falls asleep through the last part after his second beer.

*

Aaron veers right towards the closest overhead walkway. Jill realises she will never catch up. She decides to stay straight and capture pictures from the cycling fence ahead. She has spotted seats upon which she can stand. More guards appear over the walkway and Aaron is forced to spin around and head back along the fence line towards her. *Even better!* She snaps a couple of pictures as he approaches her, intent on his task.

Aaron dashes past her, and she climbs up on a seat. She gets him in focus. He is looking up. *Strange?!* His speed drops off to a slow jog, and he suddenly darts up the fence like a squirrel. She starts snapping. Aaron has seen a projectile mid-air and climbs to the fence top. The Colombian cyclist, three hours into a six-hour race, has no idea of what is about to occur; he is looking ahead, not up to the sky.

The projectile takes out his front wheel, and Jill gets the shot just as he lands in the Italian's lap. The Italian crashes badly into the rider alongside, initiating a machine gun domino effect right across the track. Cyclists behind have nowhere to go. They slam into the mess in front. It is a bike crash of epic proportions involving flying trapeze artists and dozens of bikes.

Aaron jumps the fence, hits the ground at a run, and has to jump straight back against the wire, as a wheel whizzes by him.

TIM: *Oh my God, Kym.*

KYM: *Any God will do, Tim.*

Aaron hotfoots it to the mishap and is first on the scene. People are injured. Aaron tiptoes through and over them. He rolls the Indonesian over to check for food underneath. All the cyclist can do is groan. "Sorry about that," Aaron apologises.

He lifts the Colombian's leg that is hopelessly tangled in the Italian's bike and sweeps his hand beneath him, explaining, "In a hurry."

"*Aye Puta!*" [Son of a bitch!] The cyclist spits at him.

"Learn to ride, fool. You ruined my race," yells the Italian cyclist.

The Colombian reacts badly to the insult and shouts back. More join in the blame game, and soon everyone is pointing fingers and screaming at each other. It turns into a pride hurt, amphetamine-stimulated, testosterone-injected, shit-fight.

Aaron ignores it all and continues to dig for food amongst the mayhem, even as the Frenchman unloads a torrent of insults on him.

At the same time as the chaos is occurring on the cycle track, Mr Weeks' personal assistant is poised over a security radio and announces, "Sir, his trainer is on the track looking for food."

"No. It is no longer food. It is evidence. And I want it. Do you hear me?" Mr Weeks blasts him.

Back at the melee, a chorus of obscenities and curses in a dozen different tongues are hurled at Aaron like darting arrows. Each time he raises a limb or moves a body, a new profanity in a new language is added.

He notes that medics are arriving in bands. *I'm running out of time!* He looks left and right along the track and sees guards approaching from both directions. Desperate now, he dives into the last pile of calamity with the Turkish rider on top. He dives all the way to his armpit. The song of derision and foul language is deafening. But this time, he feels something hard and not metallic amongst them. It doesn't seem attached to anyone, so he grabs it.

The guards are nearly upon him now, but it is too late. He has what he wants, and he pulls free and bolts to the fence on the far side. He leaps halfway up it, pulls himself the rest of the way over, and jumps from the top. Once on the residential side of the track, Aaron legs it like he is the one going for a gold medal.

*

A panting Aaron taps fast and hard on the balcony door of the New Zealand apartment. Guards arrive at the front of his building, and he ducks down behind the greenery. The flower angels of a tropical tetramicra orchid hang over him as he hides behind its long leaves. Impatiently, he taps again from his knees. The door slides open.

He springs up to a stoop, not quite high enough to be called a common slouch, and whispers, "Can you look after my yam?"

Nobody has ever knocked on Vincent's door and asked him to look after a yam before. He is a little bewildered, "Cuz, that's a yucca!"

Aaron is shocked. It is the first time he has heard Vincent speak. But he doesn't have time. He shoves the yucca into Vincent's chest and pushes him back behind the curtains. His mission accomplished, he leaps over the balcony rail and is gone in a flash. Vincent is left puzzled, but he closes the door and pulls the curtains shut.

*

Behind the track fence, an Irish athlete stands with a Croatian. He is not close by her, nor does she know him. She finished her event two hours ago, and his does not start until the evening. However, they both stand when they see Manohar with his pockets turned out.

Billy is slumped in a seat, with a second guard crouched before him, rummaging through his sports bag. Still soaked wet with sweat, he looks too exhausted to object. Helen is turning in tight little circles, speaking on the phone.

"You've already won! He's all cramped up. He can't go on."

"I am afraid it is out of my hands when it comes to security. They must be allowed to do their job and collect evidence. I can only advise you to cooperate." Mr Weeks' voice is coming across loud and clear on speaker, giving a green light, and a smirk, to the guard in charge.

Helen hangs up.

"Hey! What the feck ya think ya doin'?" The Irish athlete yells. "You don't look like Search and feckin' Rescue to me." She gets the attention of both guards. She also gives them a lot of unwanted attention from nearby trainers and runners. Heads turn at this latest spectacle.

"You have no right to put your fingers in an athlete's kit," the Croatian yells. "You could be fiddling with our medication. Drugs are legal here, remember?"

The guards are already satisfied that the Wongii Team has no food; there is no point in beginning a confrontation. They walk away across the field with all the urgency of choosing a spot to picnic. Billy's jaw is clenched, and the hunger and all the rage that comes with it return in one grizzly belly moan.

He looks across to the fellow athletes who have spoken up for him: a wave and a little acknowledgement are all it takes to spur him on further.

Then, although he is still shaky from exhaustion, Billy stands and pulls out a practice shot putt from the sports bag. Manohar tries to stop him, but Billy is having none of it.

"I only have to throw this once, and they can't kick me out. And I'm going to make sure this one counts."

Manohar takes it from him and follows him.

*

The anvil arms and barrel chest of the Belarus contender have seen him right. He knows it is a good throw. He waits with a big smile for confirmation from the adjudicators: 2 cm better than the world record. He punches into the air in triumph and runs to his coach and trainer with arms wide for a celebratory hug. The years of training and submitting himself to drugs have all been worth it.

The rules are clear. You only have thirty seconds from when your name is called until you have to throw the shot put. It is to be tucked in under the jawline and has to touch the neck, at all times. It is never allowed to fall below the shoulder line for this to be considered cheating and will result in disqualification.

But with a neck the breadth of his head, it is difficult for the Samoan. He has no jawline. Deltoids, the size of speed humps in a shopping centre carpark, do not help. He spends twenty-three of his thirty seconds just getting it into an acceptable position. But when he does, he smashes the new record by half a metre and makes the man from Belarus cry.

Billy's name is called. He takes the 7.26-kilogram ball and steps into the circle. With a quick glance to where he wants the shot to go, he steps to the rear of the circle and turns his back. Placing the cannon ball against his neck and above the shoulder, Billy pictures the face of the smirking security guard. He rocks back and forth, spins on the ball of his left foot, with his right slightly extended like a figure skater to build torque and brings it back in for the final push. He heaves and howls out a groan of rage as he gives it all he has. The ball sails into the air, taking all his frustration and the last of his stamina with it. It isn't his best performance, but it isn't his worst either. No one pays any attention, anyway.

The screen behind Tim and Kym's commentary is busy showing the bike crash replays from different angles. Who hit who first, and whose foot belonged to whom, mattered according to which helmet or bike it struck. Billy's shot putt effort is relegated to a small, titbit corner box of the screen.

TIM: *And after the clean-up, questions are being asked why? What exactly was being protested?*

The ticker tape running at the bottom of the screen shows Billy's position moving from 59th to 69th.

*

Billy returns with a shrug and a grin. He feels a lot better now that he has that out of his system. He isn't going back for a second or third attempt; he does not think he has the energy to improve on what he has done. Instead, he just wants to lay down and sleep. The only thing that matters right now is that he has finished the day by answering questions. He deserves to be here. *Let's see them compete with hunger pains instead of steroids!* He thinks, crowing to himself.

"Not giving in under extreme circumstances. I guess I can work with that." Helen grins with admiration.

"Gotta work with what you got," sniffs Billy. "Any sign of Aaron?"

"No. I hope I haven't got him into any trouble."

"Oh, he loves a bit of trouble," Billy assures her with a knowing smile.

*

The three guards are spread out along the street and walk it in a hurry. Aaron strolls around the corner ahead of them, whistling. They converge on him like prison guards preventing a riot from beginning. He stops and waits for them. But when they surround him, he puts his hands above his head.

"Whoa!"

The guards start their inspection with slow circling steps. Round and round they strut, trying to intimidate him. They are like sharks looking him over to see if he is edible. Dressed in shorts and a t-shirt, it is quite obvious he has no food on him. Aaron looks over his shoulder, catching the eye of one guard. He then sticks his bottom out and struggles to look down to his own bum.

"Nice, isn't it?" He mocks.

He brings his hands down to his hips and turns around to face the man. "But you have to be prepared to put in the effort. The hours," Aaron lectures. "Really work at it. Know what I mean?"

The guard stops circling and glares back. "Smart arse."

Brimming with arrogance, Aaron tilts his head and smiles back defiantly. It is a standoff until another guard speaks out. "Let's go. He's got nothing."

The man hesitates, but he complies.

CHAPTER 14

ONCE PEELED, WITH great care so as not to go too deep, it weighs in a little under a kilo of fibrous starch. Lifting the lid, steam wafts through the kitchen, and Allisante begins clapping when Rob finally removes it from the pot.

Billy's stomach growls in anticipation, having been woken up by the smell. The New Zealanders and the Wongii Troupe gather at the table of the NZ apartment surrounding Billy like they are at a birthday party waiting for the candles to be blown out on the cake. Everyone cheers when the guest of honour cuts into his birthday yucca.

"Should I save some for the morning?"

"Fuck no!" Mikey squeals in dismay. "They are calling it evidence, and this is Guantanamo Bay. Eat it all, and the plate."

"I am so happy," Allisante trills.

"I don't want anyone down on the beach after what we just saw," Helen cautions. "Do you really want to do this to yourself again tomorrow?"

"A second day will take a toll on his body," agrees Manohar.

"I don't know what that Frenchman said to me, but I'll never be able to look at a croissant again. You had better make it worth it, man," Aaron encourages.

Billy laughs. "Once I eat and sleep, I'm good."

"Well, let's keep a low profile, and go to sleep early," advises Helen. "I don't want to give them any opportunities. You can't disappoint men like Weeks. And I'm afraid I need a whole new plan now."

"I am so happy," Allisante reminds everyone.

*

Billy sleeps the kind of sleep where dreams cannot enter. A solid, all-encompassing body slumber that has no interest in what his subconscious has to say. Once he had eaten nearly a kilo, his exhausted body devoted the last of its energy in digesting the yucca and left none for Allisante or the others. He feels heavier, sinking into the lounge alongside Allisante, and his eyes soon grow drowsy.

He is the first to wake up though, and he is happy to just lay in bed. He extends his legs straight, pulls his toes back to stretch his calf muscles, and smiles at the ceiling: *I'm still here, I'm still in it!*

Not wanting to dwell on having no breakfast, he rises and takes a shower while the others sleep. The apartment is so small that the shower wakens everybody, and they are all up when he exits the bathroom. They are quiet and he thinks they all have a look of trepidation about them. It is like an unease about what is ahead, or in what to say.

"Light yoga?" He asks Manohar.

"Indeed." Manohar jumps to his feet. "But a short one. Be back in forty minutes," he advises Helen and they skip out the door.

Upon returning, Aaron and Helen have showered and are ready.

Billy takes another shower while his team eats breakfast with the New Zealanders in their apartment. He stands naked, wet, and alone, staring at his clothes that are laid out on the sink. The Wongii logo on his shorts and shirt remind him of home. He thinks of his friend, Ben, his hair caked with wads of papier mâché, and the kids making giant bees. He thinks of the Picasso clown head, and the deck his dad built for the hula-hoop ring toss. A smile crosses his face at the thought of 'Hillary Clinton' being rejected by a stud breeding goat; he had his money on Freddie Mercury! He dries himself, dresses, checks the time, and knocks on the New Zealander's door. "Ready?"

The streets of the residential complex are busy with groups of people returning from training or heading out for competition. All of them gather around their particular athlete. He feels it is okay to be amongst them. There isn't a cloud in the sky.

"Take it easy out there." Helen pauses and then adds, "And I know that sounds silly."

"It's not the 400-metre. Today starts with Discus and Javelin."

"But for Wongii's sake, it's better to finish than to not. Yesterday … Just pace yourself is all I'm asking."

"We do this every Friday at the pub. Relax. These are MY events."

As they approach the hyperactive arena entrance, heads turn. Arms are raised. Fingers click and hands are waved to their colleagues. One becomes two. The twos try to outrun threes. And a proper media flurry swarms around them. They swamp on Billy like seagulls on a kid who's tripped and dropped his chips.

"Is it true that the Cuban food was intended for you?" Jill is first. It is her photographs that have broken the story to the world.

"Have you eaten since Tuesday?" Asks Channel 12.

"Did you compete without eating?" Lachlan News interjects and shouts down the Channel 12 reporter. "And are you promoting diet pills?"

Flashbulbs fire and a boom mic drops in over his head. Billy flounders for the right answers but new questions keep coming and more microphones are thrust into his face. He is backed up against Manohar.

"Please, please," Helen steps forward. "I am happy to answer all your questions, but I am afraid you will have to wait until after the Discus for Billy."

With one look she dismisses Billy and the Troupe, and he is happy to get out of there. He does not want the distraction today. He has bigger things on his mind … things for him. He has questions of his own to answer. Aaron, Manohar, and Billy escape for the first event.

This is the spotlight. The real thing, and she is in it, centre stage. The opportunity that Helen has been waiting for. It is her turn to 'play'.

"So, he is competing today?" Channel 03 asks.

"Yes, of course. Try and stop him."

"Has he eaten today?" Jill sounds concerned.

"No, he has not." Helen declares and stifles a sigh at the unfairness of it all.

*

Mr Weeks relaxes behind his desk, espresso coffee in hand. Today's events have not yet begun, and this is the first piece of real private time he has had in days. The Games, especially the opening days, demand his full attention. He has a picture of his son at graduation— standing, without oxygen, and with a girlfriend by his side—at his fingertips, as he listens to him on loudspeaker.

"Norway is great. It has some of the most beautiful and easy walks—"

"Don't overdo it, son." Mr Weeks smiles at the thought but plays the part of a concerned parent.

"I feel fine. And I have Tati and friends looking out for me. That's what I wanted to talk to you about, Dad. Is there any chance I can delay the next checkup by a week?"

"That's not how this works, I'm sorry. You are lucky to get this medication at all," Mr Weeks reminds him. "It is still experimental."

"I know, but—"

A loud knock on the door interrupts their online chat, as Mr Weeks' personal assistant bursts in. "Sir, you will want to see this," He points to the TV.

He flicks the remote control, and Helen appears on screen. Mr Weeks has to look twice, to realise what is happening, before he jumps to his feet.

ON SCREEN:

"Do you think it is irresponsible to compete at this level without food?" A Channel 07 reporter asks.

"Let me clarify." Helen is magnanimous. "Billy did not eat before competition yesterday, nor has he eaten today. However, last night he ate an organic yucca. He has an amazing reserve tank from his all natural Wongii diet. And that's what you should be focusing on today."

She pauses for effect. "How our chemical free Billy stacks up."

"Dad?" The sound of his son's voice jolts Mr Weeks back.

"It's a trial drug, son." There is a stressful titter. "We made this deal. Sorry, I have to go." He hangs up and devotes his full attention to Helen.

"So, what happened to his food? And where did the yucca come from?" Channel 03 again.

"It was simply lost between islands. We thank the Games Management, who have been outstanding in trying to track our cargo," Helen shrugs; she is full of grace. "But no one is expected to cater for the diet we choose. Last night was an act of faith in Cuba's 'home delivery' service. *Muchos gracias*, Cuba!" She grins.

"There is currently an investigation into yesterday's incident. Did you have prior knowledge?" Jill queries.

"Are you withholding any evidence?" the Lachlan News reporter demands. "The people have a right to know."

"We have no more food, if that's what you are asking. And no prior knowledge. As for an investigation? Well, Mr Weeks has bent over backwards to help us. And I am sure he would agree: the idea of evidence having an expiration date is just ludicrous."

"Ahrrrr!" Mr Weeks roars and hurls a vase from his desk. It smashes against a framed picture of him shaking hands with a US General. Glass and vase shatter across the wall and floor, and the general falls amongst the debris. Weeks storms out of the office, his personal assistant in tow.

*

The sixth event on the card, and to begin the day, is Discus. Billy goes through his warm-up with Aaron alongside, joking that what they need now is a good-sized diamond python. He twists and stretches behind the net, as contestants take to the circle in front, one by one. There are no nerves. No worries. No concern about the lack of food. No consideration that the field and odds are stacked against him. It is just him, and that is enough.

"You can't out power this lot, Bill. You can only outperform," prompts Aaron. "Technique and more technique."

Billy thinks it is probably the best advice Aaron has ever given. His name is called, and he steps up to the circle.

Legs apart, knees bent and forward, arms extended like a scarecrow, Billy twists his torso and brings the disc to his left hand twice before commencing. You could run a level over his movements like an ocean horizon. He spins on the ball of his left foot, sweeping his right into a leap that would take the eye of the Bolshoi Ballet. His landing is gentle and momentary as he passes the momentum back to his left foot and rotates his body into the throw. His fingers release the disc automatically and without a thought.

> TIM: *Beautiful to watch, Kym. But at sixty-seven metres, he just lacks a good dose of steroids.*

> KYM: *Or even a bone to chew on from media reports, Tim! But the kid's got something. He moves back up to 59th place.*

Helen arrives to join the others trackside with a spring in her step. She is invigorated. It has been so long since she felt satisfied. Not in her city job of the last few years, certainly not in the extra work she put into her home office, nor the mishmashed ethereal workings of Wongii.

On his second throw, Billy repeats his first effort with all the grace and poise of an Audrey Hepburn rerun at a Sex Pistols concert. It is

Audrey-esque with her back straight, elegantly dressed in black and pearls, brimming with manners … and Sid Vicious spitting on the front row. Billy betters the Australian record by one centimetre.

TIM: *Just imagine what this kid could do with a cocktail of testosterone and amphetamines.*

KYM: *I have no idea what his hormone situation is, but I want some!*

Helen's phone beeps. She has been waiting for it. She has been expecting the call as soon as the news broke in Wongii. It worries her a little, but she could not break the news herself; it would have been a betrayal to Billy. She takes a deep breath and prepares herself for Zoom-time.

"Hi Janine."

*

In the Buckman kitchen, Jack and Dale have just finished lunch, and it is 'beer o'clock'. Janine had been on the laptop all morning.

"What on earth is going on?" Janine asks in a puzzled voice. "Our webpage suddenly has a million followers. And they are all saying he hasn't eaten."

"Try not to worry. He is in good health this morning and eager to go." Helen tries her best to allay Janine's fears with her 'calming voice'.

"It's this afternoon that I'm worried about," Dale chimes in.

"What happened to the food we packed? Are the bags lost?" Janine asks.

"Nothing is lost. It was taken." Helen explains. "Our kitchen was cleaned out as well. It's Management."

"Bastards!" Dale yells, banging his beer on the table.

"Disgraceful!" Shrieks Janine, thinking not just of Billy, but of her son.

Jack hears a thud from the next room and squeezes his eyes shut. He just knows it is Rubi the goat, stressed by the loud voices. He seems to be the only one who has heard it though, and that annoys him even more.

"And you're being nice to them? You should be jumping up and down to the press." There is a new tone in her voice. One Helen has not heard before. A tone of anger.

Jack leaves the kitchen to follow the sound of the thud. Dale has known Jack for over fifty years, and he thinks it looks more like sneaking away.

"We can't make this, 'Us vs Them' … they will drag us into court, and we can't afford it. We need to focus on Billy's choices. Don't let them distract us. This is a whole new race, and we need to stay in it, as long as we can, and get what we can."

"Is there anything we can do? And who is the Cuban girl?" Janine asks.

Dale finds Jack in the living room holding two goat legs. He is dragging Rubi out from behind the sofa where she was eating a pair of his socks. "Why are you so quiet? What's going on?"

"Your goat's not funny anymore," declares Jack, leaving Rubi in peace.

"Don't play games with me. You don't seem surprised."

"Well, a cheater's gotta cheat," Jack philosophises. "And they don't want any 'Vegan Invasion' next games, do they? They'll do whatever it takes and call it 'Risk Management'."

"So, you knew something like this would happen?"

"Na, not his food. I thought he'd get bribed. Or knocked down, and we'd get free publicity. Something along those lines."

"So, you sent him over there to get knocked down?" Janine's loud voice startles both of the men. "This was all your idea, Dad!"

"Oh, he always gets back up," is Jack's excuse.

Janine digs her hands into her hair, turns around, and storms out, "Argh!"

"You're a bloody monster," Dale shakes his head and also exits the room.

"Baaahh!" Rubi clunks to her feet. Her hooves tap along the floorboards as she follows Dale and Janine into the kitchen.

Billy Uke is born on social media on a Tuesday night. No one has ever really died on social media, but many have been birthed with an unknown or unwanted pregnancy. It is just good or bad luck, and simply, "Good morning, here you are! Welcome to the world of no reason."

This phenomenon happens instantaneously, and it is everywhere. It slides straight into podcast and talkback radio, makes its way to current affairs television, and is in print by the time Billy has picked up the discus.

—In South Africa, a street party is taking place. Music blares and beer flows in the evening heat. One reveller holds her phone out as she dances and sends a message to Billy: "*All the best from Cape Town.*" Half the street begins to cheer: "Never give up, brother," her dance partner cries.

—In central Australia, in a scene of epic desert beauty, a group of Koori teenagers hold up black and white, A4 photocopied pictures of Billy.

"Woo hoo, we are with you Billy!" Amanda hollers.

"Yeah, we are with you," Jimmy waves his photocopy about. "You're deadly, brother."

"We're starting a fan club for you," Kristina tells him.

—On a Sydney train station, two labourers wait for the 6.00 am to Central Station. One is reading the Lachlan Press newspaper, of which the headline reads: 59th Placed Loser Tells Us How to Eat!

"It's the Drug Games, for fuck's sake. If this hypocrite doesn't agree with Steroids, he shouldn't be there."

—On the streets of Perth, Western Australia, a Climate Change/Extinction protest is underway. A woman in her thirties with a nose piercing wears a t-shirt with Billy's face printed on it. An ABC journalist stops her for an interview.

"Billy Uke represents the viability of sustainable food practice. I don't care about the Games; he is already a winner in my book."

—In London, on a panel TV show of Current Affairs, Mr Davies, in his expensive suit and wearing a cravat, speaks to Cynthia.

"I actually have sympathies. He's from a minority; clearly disadvantaged. Even naïve. And I for one, find it appalling that the Left would take advantage of the poor chap."

Cynthia, from Nigerian descent, looks over her glasses. "But you still haven't answered my question. By what right, is the US even in Cuba?"

—At an undisclosed home studio somewhere in mid-state USA, two shock jocks sit beneath a confederate flag and a portrait of a bald eagle. Both are in their forties, both are overweight, and both are dressed like models from a Cabellos Catalogue Fall Edition, in their matching camouflage outfits.

"The Games are supposed to be free of politics. I mean, these people even hate sport!" Decries the first.

"Typical. They want everything equal until you give it to them. Fucking Lib-tards." Shouts the second.

Billy is unaware of any of this.

CHAPTER 15

THE SEVENTH EVENT of the decathlon is Javelin, and hunger has returned in earnest. It is 11 am and seventeen hours since he has eaten. He pushes it aside and concentrates on the task at hand, as he waits on the sideline with Aaron. They are watching the Canadian run in for his throw when some of the media catches up with him.

"And how are you feeling today?" A Spanish reporter asks.

"I feel good. Happy with Discus and looking forward to the Javelin."

"We expect to do well in Javelin," Aaron butts in. "It's a Friday fixture in Wongii, along with cross-country running. Probably his strongest events."

"Is that right? A fixture?" An Australian reporter from Channel 13 queries.

"Yeah. All takers. Come on down." Billy puts out the invitation.

*

Without knocking, Mr Weeks storms into a plush corporate lounge box unlike any other. It is larger than any other and the curtains are closed, darkening the room; a multitude of screens cover the walls. It is empty, save for an eighty-year-old man, finely dressed, who is sitting before a silver tray of nibbles with a coffee in hand. He is sitting in an enormous lounge with his Personal Assistant standing in the corner in front of the air conditioner; her dress is fluttering in its breeze. She is holding an iPad in her hands. Mr Weeks' personal assistant, however, stops at the open doorway. He does not want to enter.

"I thought we had a deal," Mr Weeks hollers.

"I'm sorry. It was not something I planned for." The statement is in earnest. But a wry grin appears. A chuckle follows. "The thing seems to have gotten a life of its own once pictures got out. It simply became news."

"These are multi-million-dollar contracts. 'I'm sorry' doesn't cut it!" Mr Weeks is not amused.

"Fuck off, Weeks, I don't answer to you." The Mogul's grin disappears. Serious and surly, he puts his coffee cup down. "I AM the media, for Christ's sake. How does … 'Weeks Gets Gold—as an Inside Trader' sound for a headline?"

Mr Weeks shoots a guilty look at the man's personal assistant. She lowers her head and looks at the floor. His jaw clenches, his teeth gnash, and he returns a hateful gaze to the Media Mogul. The Mogul is unmoved. He picks up his coffee cup and takes a sip. Mr Weeks' personal assistant steps back from the doorway. Mr Weeks turns around and storms back out.

*

Billy has stretched out his hamstrings, and his upper body, and with the javelin in both hands, he holds it high above his head, skipping along sideways in practice, at the back of the field. Billy is feeling good, he is feeling confident, the one thing he is not feeling is intimidated. Not anymore. That has passed.

"No stress, brother, let it flow. Your footwork is good. Just remember to get that elbow up high and let it flow," Aaron instructs.

He flexes his wrist while watching the Nigerian. He flexes his fingers back while watching the Norwegian break the Olympic record.

He doesn't care. And when his name is called, he bounces the javelin from one hand to the other like he owned it.

He sets off in his run, keeping the spear tip up and level, and where he can see it. Pulling his arm way back, Billy canters into his crossover footwork, five steps in all. He is much looser in his style than the other competitors. More fluid. On his final step, Billy flings his elbow forward and high with all his weight and momentum behind it. He whips his wrist, whips his fingers, and the javelin rolls off them in a beautiful spin. Billy watches it sail away to a Personal Best of 88.7 metres; it is just shy of the Australian national record. He now has a new goal for his next two throws: to better himself.

The representative from Trinidad is in an epic battle with the Chilean Grasshopper. They leapfrog each other in their attempts, smashing world records along the way, trying to be the first ever to throw 100-metres.

In Billy's second attempt, he pushes it. He thinks about his actions, about everything he is doing and the perfect timing of each motion … but he tries too hard. The javelin goes wide to the right and falls a half metre shorter than his first.

He knows what he has done wrong. He knew it the moment the javelin left his hand. Taking a seat to wait for his final attempt, Billy closes his eyes, regulates his breathing, and leaves it all behind. Dwelling on failure, or even disappointment, is the enemy of moving ahead. It carries more weight than a sack of potatoes; that is something that Jack has taught him. He has to be himself, relax, and listen to Aaron—*Let it flow.*

Billy's third attempt is not just loose, it is unorthodox. Others call it sloppy. He skips into his crossover footwork like a double beat salsa song, and when he brings his arm from behind, torso and shoulder in sync, he raises his elbow high. However, the elbow is not straight up, directly in line with his body. Instead, it is out to the side somewhat, but it feels more natural. It is what his body wants to do, and it is the least path of resistance.

From the elbow to the wrist to the fingers, his arm flings out like a trebuchet. The energy flows into the javelin, sending it flying high. It does not break the Finnish national record, nor the USA, Swedish, or a half dozen other countries' records. But it does break his Personal Best and the Australian record.

*

The television coverage now shows full screen shots of Billy. No longer relegated to corner boxes sharing the screen with other athletes, or comparisons with thigh sizes of Grasshoppers and Kenyans, Billy *is* the story. It displays his attempt in its entirety, from his lead-in run to his grin afterwards when the javelin has landed.

> KYM: *It may be far short of the leaders, but that is two Personal Bests in a row.*

> TIM: *Still early in the day, but Billy Uke looks strong.*

The screen crosses over to world events showing the fallout from the day before and the breach of the Guantanamo Bay fence. The US Secretary of State speaks at a podium about the need for US Security. It then crosses over to the current street march taking place in Havana regarding the 60-year embargo of Cuba. Thousands are rallying with placards listing the twelve US presidents that have failed to change anyone's mind over fifteen elections. Or pointing out the annual resolution passed every year at the United Nations General Assembly since 1992 to demand its end.

> TIM: *But as the US government issues a 'Please explain' notice to Cuba, questions are being asked, Kym. How do we know the food was organic? And would it indeed be classified evidence?*

> KYM: *The avocados were wrapped in spinach, with love, Tim. Where has the love gone?*

*

All competitors have enjoyed a series of snacks during the morning to keep their demanding energy levels up. After the Javelin event, they stop for a very calibrated lunch. Nothing too heavy, for Pole Vault is next on the card and nobody wants to be heavier than they already were… or make a mess on the track.

Billy has to make do with Mikey's South Island 'magic water'. He is famished now, and his stomach will not let him forget. It growls and bays at him.

The mid-afternoon heat is again starting to show on athletes and spectators alike with people fanning themselves, their clothes wet from perspiration.

Billy has stretched out, is loosening up when the athletes return from lunch, and physically, muscle-wise, he was ready. But Aaron can sense his friend is lagging in energy and enthusiasm. His confidence and drive have dropped off during the break, and he now appears a little dull and lethargic.

At the edge of the track, as Billy departs for the field, Aaron thinks it better to downplay it all and allay some of his fears. "All you have to do is remember what Grandpa says: 'It's a long jump. Let the pole do the work.'"

To the chagrin of a few athletes, those who have indulged in the need to intimidate their opponent or 'psych them out', Billy lowers the bar to a height with which he is confident. Sniggers can be heard behind his back. He reminds himself that any result is better than a 'No Result' … and that is a very real possibility the way he is feeling. His stomach will not shut up.

Billy locates his grip on the pole, pictures his success, and sets off. Holding the pole by his hip with one hand and pointing the other end to the sky, he sprints down the track. He allows it to drop down as he approaches the bar, strikes the tip into the box and pitches himself forward. The pole lifts him up to the bar. He floats over it and pushes the pole away. It is an easy jump. He splashes upon the mat to no fanfare, but it has brought him a smile and a sense of relief.

On his second attempt, he surpasses his first with a 5.8 metre. Most of the field has recorded 5.9 metre, and half are now above the 6-metre mark. Try as he might, Billy cannot outdo his second attempt and he clips the bar on his following vaults.

TIM: *Another win in mediocrity there, Kym, in what can only be described as a self-inflicted diet.*

KYM: *Nothing mediocre about it to his growing fan base. He must be starving by now, Tim.*

TIM: *Not so the Chilean Grasshopper. At six foot seven, well fed, and a pole nine inches longer than his opponents, he has his eye on beating his own world record.*

The Grasshopper limbers up, eyeing down the track to the high bar like it is an enemy target. His coach hands him the pole and gives him his final pep talk: "*El Campion. Eres el Saltamontes. Puedes volar!*" [The champion. You are the Grasshopper. You can fly.]

The coach reaches into his pocket and produces the final secret weapon for the Pole Vault world record. He steps in close and snaps a cap of amyl nitrate under the Grasshopper's nose.

His eyes widen like a nocturnal bug hunter in an Indonesian rainforest: "*Puedo volar.*" [I can fly.]

Heart racing, blood pumping, the Grasshopper sets off down the track in long, ever-increasing strides. He focuses on the box ahead, aiming his pole at the pit, plants it square, and launches himself with his magnificent thighs. But on the commencement, he has jumped too high, dissipating the forward momentum.

The pole straightens before it is fully upright, and when it reaches the highest point, the Grasshopper tilts upside down, legs in the air, with not enough follow through. Everyone feels it. There is a sickening anticipation. That choking of the chest when a child is falling, and you can't quite catch them in time. Everyone except Aaron. "Yeah! He said long jump."

The Grasshopper totters upside down in a long, excruciating, balancing act. It proves to be futile. The pole begins to lean away from the mat and back toward the direction from which he had come. Ever so slowly at first, the speed picks up exponentially as he follows the 7-metre arc of his pole back to the unforgiving hard track. A loud 'snap' rings out through the stadium. The Grasshopper lets out a sickly scream and is left writhing about holding a leg that is bent sideways below the knee.

> KYM: *Errr, and that's a sound no one wants to hear; like a Christmas cracker at a bar mitzvah.*

> TIM: *Horrible scene. Chilean dreams of greatness shattered.*

> KYM: *Career ending, I'd say ... but on the bright side, it does make this field competitive again.*

Photographers from around the world hone in on the Chilean with their long lenses, trying to get the 'The Face of Pain' shot, the 'End Of The Road' shot, and the 'Icarus was a Grasshopper' shot.

*

Like everyone else in the stadium and around the world, the Wongii Team watch horrified at the Grasshopper's plight. Out of nowhere, the Gotta-Aid Executive Helen has been avoiding steps in to join them. He holds up official-looking paperwork and Helen flushes with anxiety.

"Hello, Helen. I have the contract ready." He smiles full of confidence and appears relaxed, as if he belonged there.

"What contract? Who are you?" Billy reaches for the contract, but Helen snatches at it first.

"Gotta-Aid. We have a sponsorship deal beginning the second day," the executive declares, extending his hand to greet Billy. He brushes it aside.

"We do not have a deal," Helen blasts.

"You've been speaking to him behind our backs?" Billy cries.

"We spoke. That was all." She gives a look of thunder to the executive.

"We do recognise the publicity you have already gained for our client," the executive prompts, "I thought maybe—?"

"You thought wrong." Helen cuts him off. She crumples the contract into a little ball and forces it back into his hand. "I just needed a press pass off you. Get out of here."

The executive's brow creases, and he looks from Billy to Helen, confused. "Okay, okay," he shrugs his shoulder and backs away.

"He called me his client."

"It's not like that." Helen's face flushes red and a feeling of guilt crashes upon her. She pauses before speaking, choosing her words very carefully. "I only promised him that I 'planned' to talk with him," she explains, making the quotation sign with double fingers.

Billy, Aaron, and Manohar look sceptical. They shake their heads and give each other an expression of 'lousiest excuse ever'.

Walking away, the Gotta-Aid Executive smiles like he's been dealt four aces in a poker tournament. It is a job well done. He looks across at Mr Daniels, the Security Chief, who is watching on from a discrete distance. A long lens camera is in hand, that he now lowers as he gives his nod of approval to the executive.

*

It is another hour until the 110-metre hurdles begin. It is the ninth and final event of the day. It is a very long and uncomfortable hour for the Wongii Squad. It is unbearably humid this late in the day and Helen feels that she is in a spotlight she wants turned off. Her team has stopped talking and Billy has sunk into a world of his own.

There are enough products around here. Bright coloured, shitty, cleverly worded, unsound, unhinged, expensive, detrimental, bullshit things. *I am not a fucking product!* He reasons with himself. He has always found it strange seeing elite soccer players being sold to other clubs for the highest bidder, like a cow at the market: fenced in with no say. *The ancient Greeks and Spartans had it right; no shoes and no excuses. Do it naked. Show me what you got, don't tell me. I am not a fucking cow!*

Billy is not simply disappointed in Helen for not keeping him informed; he is angry. He feels that he has been betrayed. He can't bring himself to look at her. He feels he is alone. The constant, gnawing irritation of hunger amplifies it all and drowns out reason. When his time comes to take to the field, he kicks the sports bag, sending water bottles flying on his departure. Helen jumps in her seat.

Across the field, standing between the long-legged Kenyan and the Samoan powerhouse, Billy has never been so motivated.

The line-up falls to their hands: some are arching their backs up high, others lying low and forward to give calf muscles a final stretch.

Placing their feet in the starting blocks, they adjust and readjust each foot's placement to get the perfect position. They drop one knee to the track and inch their fingers back across the line, spreading them wide, as the starter picks up the gun. "On your mark."

Burning anger ignites what fuel Billy has left before the starter makes his second call. "Get set."

The athletes raise their knees and are in position. His heart is already racing.

BANG! They spring out of the blocks in perfect unison.

One hurdle. Two hurdles, and the line is even. Three, and the Kenyan inches ahead. On the fourth, the field begins to break up with the Kenyan taking a stronger lead. Billy throws himself over a hurdle and remains with the second row of runners. The fifth sees the genius shot putting Samoan misstep on his landing. He manages to keep up with Billy to the sixth hurdle, running at a forty-five-degree angle, arms flailing about, but he cannot lift his huge frame. He crashes through it and takes it with him.

By the seventh, there is no more blood glucose left to stimulate

Billy's muscles and they fire on adrenaline alone. The Kenyan winning is a foregone conclusion, and the athlete from Sierra Leone creeps ahead of the second line of runners. After the eighth hurdle, Billy is still a contender for third along with Canada and Jamaica.

At the ninth, his adrenaline proves no match for the sustained durability of steroids and amphetamines. Billy wills himself over the final hurdle but the Jamaican edges ahead and the Canadian pips him on the line. He finishes a breathtaking fifth with only centimetres between them.

Past the line, runners ease off to a walk. The winner continues in a triumphant jog, hands in the air down the track. Billy struggles for breath and is at a stop with his hands on his knees. The Canadian wanders back to stand by him and the Jamaican returns to pat him on the back.

KYM: *Monumental effort by the native Australian, Tim.*

TIM: *Indeed, indeed. But a marked difference on the body between Discus and Hurdles, Kym. He has, however, completed his day on a reserve tank.*

KYM: *Still, the world wants to know, is this the last we see of Billy Uke?*

*

Billy lumbers back, drenched in sweat. It drips from his nose and runs from his fingers. He slumps into a chair.

"Holy shit, I thought you were going to pull off a place there," Aaron declares.

"Congratulations. Rest." Manohar gives him a fresh water bottle.

"Oh, well done. You finished the day strong," Helen congratulates, clapping. "On a reserve tank! Wongii is in the news. Calls are coming in from everywhere, and I have interviews lined up for tonight. Let's get you showered, fed, and roll you out to the press."

"Fed? Let's wait and see how I feel in the morning."

"No. No, I cannot allow that again. It is not safe," says Manohar, shaking his head rigorously.

"We can't be hypocritical with health," agrees Helen. "It is not a good look having you collapse three kilometres into the Cross-Country race. It risks everything."

"Unless you have another side deal, I am not aware of," Billy swings his head to stare at Helen. "One for me NOT to finish! I want my chance."

"That's not fair," Helen states huffily, hurt by his implication. "It's not like that." But Billy does not back down, instead he stands and faces off with her and Manohar, hunger and anger taking over.

Manohar has never seen Billy like this. He has known him to be a considerate, affable soul who always sees the best in people. "There is no shame in not finishing." Manohar articulates every word with compassion, but he is clear in his conviction, "It is the reasonable thing to do without food, and the ethical example to set."

"Absolutely. To your fan base, you have already won," nods Helen.

"No, YOU have won. You have what YOU want. I am nine events into ten!" The comment is in a raised voice and pointed, as he stares at Helen. His attention then switches to Manohar, "And I came here to compete. Whether YOU think it is reasonable to you or not!"

There is a long, uncomfortable pause before Manohar speaks. "And I came here to be a medic. I am no one's water-boy." He throws the sports bag at Billy's feet, steps past him, and marches away.

Allisante arrives full of bounce and bubble to congratulate Billy, "Hola everybody."

"Manohar?" Helen calls out. "Manohar, please come back."

"Well done mate," says Aaron. "Way to say thanks for coming!" He steps over the bag and walks past Billy towards the apartment block.

Helen bends down to recover the bag.

"Leave it." Billy snaps, refusing to look at her. She backs away. The last thing she wants is to escalate the situation. Instead, she pulls her lips in, raising her eyebrows to Allisante, and opens her eyes wide, hoping she can read her face and know that right now, Allisante is very much needed. She then leaves and follows Aaron.

Billy picks up the bag before Allisante can make a decision to. Together, they dawdle far behind Helen and Aaron in a disturbing, tense silence. The dejected group exit the stadium, cross the practice fields for the streets, and still a word is not said between them. Reaching the apartment building, Billy has hardly raised his head.

He holds the door open for Allisante as they enter the foyer, and she notices Helen glance over her shoulder and press the elevator button as she passes it. She takes the hint.

When the elevator doors opened, Allisante steers Billy in and leads him to the back wall. He leans against it, feels its coolness and drops the bag. She presses button number eight to the top floor and joins alongside him, leaning on the wall. He exhales long and loud. Her hand slides across to hold his.

In the Wongii apartment, Aaron stands by the table waiting for Billy, but Helen closes the door behind her. "He needs space," she announces. "We should get ready for the interviews. You can shower first."

Aaron gathers his clothes, towel, and toiletries while Helen busies herself doing nothing of consequence other than trying to make herself look busy, waiting for him to close the bathroom door. She pulls out her phone as soon as it is shut.

Billy is not the only pressing matter on her mind. Opening her emails (Tuesday is empty), she scrolls past the forty new ones that have come in since the morning's interview, until she finds the one that has frightened her. It is one that she has been avoiding—a notification from her bank. She closes her eyes and steadies herself before opening it. It reads: *Mortgage Foreclosure Notice!*

Helen turns her phone off and slides it far away from her. She sits back in the chair and covers her face with her hands. Her fingers slip into her hair, and her face slumps down against the table.

CHAPTER 16

AFTER HIS SHOWER, Aaron makes a beeline for the cafeteria, returning with food for both him and Helen to eat in the New Zealander's apartment. With a loss of appetite, Helen only picks at hers and Aaron finishes it off on the lounge while they wait for Billy.

Helen leans back against the sink with a black coffee that Vincent has made for her without being asked; he is now wiping down the bench tops. *He really is quite meticulous and kind,* Helen thinks. She pulls back the window curtain and notices two guards have been stationed across the street. They look up at her. She doesn't like the look of that but thinks it better to keep it to herself.

"Don't worry, Helen. Manohar will be back," Aaron calls from the lounge. "There's nowhere else to go."

There is a knock at the door before a showered Billy enters with Allisante by his side. "Let's get this over with," he says curtly.

Helen puts her coffee down and leaves the kitchen, approaching the couple. "Allisante," she sighs, "I'm truly sorry. But we need to keep this about Billy and not you. Or any connection to Cuba."

Billy huffs and squirms, but Allisante grabs his arm to calm before he could object. "Helen is right. You have work to do for Wongii. I can wait here."

"Yeah, you can. It's all good," says Rob.

Billy doesn't like it, but he concedes.

*

The beaches of Cuba are something to behold, and Guantanamo Bay is no exception. Impossible white sand stretches out as far as the eye can see, separating a wall of tropical greenery from the sea. It is underlaid by a blue ocean to give it a clear, inviting, turquoise colour. Occasional coconut trees or palms dot the open sand, standing forward from a jungle that encroaches upon the water's edge as far as Mother Nature allows. It is the kind of spot where you would string a hammock if you could find two palm trees close enough together and stick your fingers in your ears when life calls you back.

The sun has cooled by now and is beginning to sink below the horizon. Three men drop their sandals in the sand, backs to the sun, and face east, laying out prayer mats on the beach. Mohammed had found solace here at the previous games, when he prepared the grounds for competition, and he has invited fellow Indonesian, Ali, to join him. Both men are forty-three years old. Mohammed is slender while Ali is thicker set, and both have spent what has felt like a lifetime working abroad sending remittance to their families. They have taken it upon themselves to look out for the younger Yusef, as it is his first time out of his Malaysian homeland.

Prayers begin. Prostrating themselves on the first bow, Manohar steps out from the jungle, huffing and puffing, carrying a large rock. Busy pushing his way through the foliage collecting rocks, he is unaware of their arrival and finds himself standing in front of three men bowing to their god. He is interrupting prayers and immediately he freezes, red-faced.

On the second bow, Manohar drops the rock and makes a hurried, clumsy retreat down the beach to where he has a small pile already stacked. Embarrassed, he thinks it best to stop what he is doing and wait by the water's edge until their prayers are finished. He decides that he can say one himself.

When prayers are completed, the men roll up their mats in silence and place them together under a coconut tree.

"Who is this idiot?" Asks Mohammed, motioning his head towards Manohar. A wry smile tells a very different story to anger and elicits a laugh out of Yusef. Anger would be unacceptable so soon after prayer and in such a peaceful setting.

"Let's find out," says Ali.

Leaving the prayer mats, the three march down the sand toward Manohar.

*

The streets have an atmosphere of buoyant delight as the Wongii Troupe make their way to the press conference. Athletes and their entourages of trainers, doctors, and management relax and go their separate ways after the day's competitions. They wander to or from parks, the cafeteria, or the clear waters of a swim dockside at the waterfront. They carry the hope of exchanging stories and meeting new people and cultures, with the prospect of sex never far away. The mad testosterone and hormone levels present demand it. But not for Billy … he is too tired.

"Tonight is important for Wongii," begins Helen. "We get time to talk about you and your connection with healthy food. Just be yourself, relax and smile."

"And when they ask about the five-kilometre Cross Country event for tomorrow?" Billy asks, his voice low and exhausted.

"Well, I think it best to leave them hanging," replies Helen. "Be non-committal. It builds interest."

"But that's not—"

"You told us you would wait until the morning to decide," she says, shutting him down before the conversation gets out of hand again. "It's what you promised, remember?"

Helen looks over her shoulder. *There they are …* It's the same two security guards she saw earlier outside their apartment, still following them. She picks up the pace.

One of the security guards looks over his shoulder. Vincent stares back. His tā moko facial tattoos are unmistakable amongst those out for an evening stroll, who are in their little groups chatting or holding hands. His eyes peel back wide, and he sticks his tongue out, letting it drop to his chin in a fierce warning. The guard taps his partner to pick up the pace.

Helen feels a lot safer when they reach the park and see the media waiting for them. *There must be thirty or forty people here,* she muses with relief. The area is bright with camera lights.

Helen gives a courteous smile to journalists and makes way for Billy to be in the centre. "Good evening, everybody. Wow, quite the—"

"Are you taking supplementary drinks over your hometown Wongii Organics?" Channel 11 jumps in and shouts at Billy above the noise.

"No."

"How long have you been in negotiations with Gotta-Aid, Miss Ellis?" Channel 04 shoots at Helen. "And was yesterday's Cuban incident a publicity stunt?"

"Of course not." Helen is offended at the question. "And we are not in any negotiations with them, or anybody else."

"But you had a contract with Gotta-Aid. Do you deny meeting with Gotta-Aid's Mr Evans?" The journalist steps forward and shows Helen and Billy images of her receiving the Gotta-Aid contract passed to her. Billy and Helen lock eyes.

Helen straightens up and stands tall. "The offer was soundly rejected."

"Is that because your price was too high?" Lachlan News baits Billy. "Is it true you asked for 'unrealistic figures', end quote?"

"That's not true." Billy raises his voice back to the man.

"Will you reveal what the figure is, then?" Channel 04 asks.

"Have you ever visited Cuba before, Miss Ellis?" Lachlan News inquires, "And are you a socialist?"

It goes on like a bare-knuckle, tag-team boxing match against the new kid in school for another ten excruciating minutes.

*

Mr Weeks and his Security Chief, Mr Daniels, sit with a scotch, enjoying the drama being played out as Helen tries to defend herself in an interview that has turned into a true press mauling.

"He's only had water since yesterday. Nobody can put on a show without food for that length of time. Not even the best drugs can help him now," Mr Daniels assures his boss.

"Running is bad. Being in the top fifty of the Decathlon without enhancement is unacceptable for our sponsors," Mr Weeks says. "God forbid he finishes in the top twenty tomorrow. Cover all contingencies and have a medical team ready in the morning. This bitch is as stubborn as a goat."

*

Helen, Aaron, and Billy shuffle down the hall like they have just been swatted into an alleyway by a dragon's tail: shocked and bruised, yet glad it is the arse end of it, so they are spared any more fire.

"Well, that went well," Aaron says caustically. "At least it answers my question of chasing fame or fortune in life." Billy gives him a 'look'.

Helen opens the door and halts, staring at a huge, over the top, fruit basket sitting on the kitchen table. She looks back at Billy and Aaron, who are open-mouthed at the bounty before them.

They hasten inside, and Helen closes the door. Aaron looks around for any more surprises. Billy opens the note that is attached, and seeing that it is addressed to Helen, passes it to her. He sits down staring at the fruit, as if in a daze, and his belly starts talking again. Helen sits and reads the card aloud.

Dear Helen,
Apologies for any inconvenience. I know quality when I see it, and the

job offer still stands. You attract more bees with honey, so name your price. We would be proud to have you onboard.
Yours sincerely,
Mr Weeks

It is not what anybody is expecting, and a pause ensues before Helen speaks rather hesitantly: "It could be organic. He may be trying to defuse the situation and look like the saviour to the media: Look! We came to the rescue."

"I'm not taking the chance," announces Billy.

"Oh, he's psyching you out, Bill," Aaron says. "He is psyching you both out. Sets you up with that Gotta-Aid clown, and now he offers a bribe. The sly prick is dividing us."

They think about Aaron's words and Billy picks up a mango. "He's right about one thing, though. You should take the job." Aaron, shaking his head, takes the fruit away from Billy.

"She kept her promise," Bill looks up at him. "We have more attention than I ever wanted." He turns to Helen. "But what about after the Games? What's next for you? It will be over, one way or the other tomorrow, because I am going to run no matter what anybody says."

His query surprises her. She not only needs a job, she also needs a way of saving her house. Instead of answering, Helen runs her hands through her hair, picks up her phone, and stares off into space without using it. They give her time to think.

She exhales, stands and drops the basket of fruit in the bin.

"But today I'm employed by Wongii," she declares. "And I agree; you can't take the chance."

Helen keeps the card, though. She holds it between her fingers and taps it on the table. "I bet they pay well … You should see his office!"

Billy and Aaron laugh.

*

During the night, Aaron gets up to use the bathroom. It is after midnight. He can see the hue of Helen's phone illuminating her room.

He stops a moment and watches her pacing around her little cell-like room. He thinks it is best to leave her in privacy. He knows that she has big decisions to make, and he doesn't envy her.

Helen is tired. Exhausted, in fact, and still a little bruised from the press mauling she has received earlier. The last thing she wants is to return home to Australia and find the locks have been changed on her door. Homeless and jobless at her age is a scary thought. She stops pacing and starts texting.

$100 000. Not tomorrow. Now.

She throws her phone on the bed. These things take time. She sits on the bed until the phone's light dims to nothing and she sits in the dark. A feeling of restlessness consumes her though, and she bounces up to begin pacing again. Twenty minutes pass and still there is no reply. *Did I ask too much? Perhaps it wasn't enough time, and I sounded desperate?*

Helen grabs the phone and checks the volume. *Maybe I missed it.* But there hasn't been a reply.

It is 1.10 am, and she has a headache when the phone chimes with a text. She dives for it.

The text message reads: *OK. Done.*

She falls upon the bed fully clothed, phone in hand, and succumbs to a deep sleep.

CHAPTER 17

GAZING DOWN AT the white sand bordered by green foliage and a turquoise ocean to the rising orange glow of sunrise was a spectacular sight. With prayers finished, mats were rolled and deposited under the same tree. The four men faced the ocean and admire the rock pool they built during the night.

After hearing Manohar's tale of Billy, the men had gathered together and scrambled through the jungle with what little light remained, as fast as they could move. They didn't bother carrying things to the water to make a pile, but rather tossed what they could find out of the jungle to gather later. Mohammed considered it the neighbourly thing to do. Yusef then ran the beach back to the complex to collect snacks, water, and two headlamps from the garbage removal facility where he was contracted.

Sticks were used as stakes and driven into the sand side by side with stones. Rocks were stacked alongside and upon each other. They scoured the jungle edge further along the beach under torchlight and piled what they found on top.

Now, with daylight spreading across the sky, Manohar checks his watch and states, "The tide is not quite low enough."

"Do we have time to wait?" Queries Yusef.

"No, we do not," replies Manohar.

"We do not," agrees Ali, unfolding and dropping his sarong to the sand. "I saw that kid in the 400-metre. He was terrible."

They toss their kufis aside and strip down to their underwear. Mohammed suddenly points out a fin breaking in the water. "We are blessed." Yusef rubs his hands together, impatient to get started.

"How will you get the fish past the guards?" Mohammed asks.

"I have not thought of that," ponders Manohar.

"I know how. Leave that to me," Ali states.

They walk down to the rock pool and spread out. There are no waves and the tide only laps at the sand in its retreat. Fish are easily visible in the clear water. Manohar enters at one end and Yusef at the other. "Do we go to the back and herd them forward?" Yusef asks.

Ali follows him into the pool, moving slow and gentle. "I don't know. But they are not sheep. I don't think they are going to comply." A fish darts past. "Did you see that?"

Mohammed creeps in from the middle and stands still, waiting for an opportunity to come his way. He is only shin deep, but he can see two fish milling around just in front of him. The sun is now high enough to cast a shadow and fish move away from them to find a safer position. The rock pool is getting smaller. Fish and fishermen hold their positions, eyeing any movement. Above the water, it looks like a blind man's Mexican standoff with the four men staring down at their feet.

A fish drifts closer to Mohammed's feet and he steadies his hands. *A little closer ... A little more.* He spears his hands down and grabs at it. "Got one!"

The fish flaps and twists as he pulls it from the water for all to see. With a frantic flap, it slips straight out of his hands. Ali dives for it, misses, and breaks the water. Visibility is lost, along with the calm, and a swarm of fish whizz by looking for escape.

Manohar lunges for one; Yusef tries to splash a couple toward Ali in the shallower water, and Mohammed tries running them to shore in the even shallower water. It is ugly, it is bedlam. It is a fisherman's nightmare.

*

Aaron and Mikey are sitting at the NZ dining table eating toast and eggs, dissing the hen, and jeering at what a super-enhanced chicken looks like.

Meanwhile, Helen leans into her hand, waiting for the second coffee pot. She has bags under her eyes that weren't there yesterday. Only sleep or more coffee can remedy that.

Billy and Allisante are in private conversation, staying away from the food, on the sunken lounge. His stomach has already started growling at the morning.

Rob walks to the table with the fresh pot and pours it. With a sniff, he breaches the subject that everyone has been avoiding. "Still no Manohar?"

Aaron shakes his head.

"Hasn't returned." Helen's eyes flick from the table to Billy.

Billy swings his head at the sound of Manohar's name. He feels terrible about how he acted the previous day. And allowing himself to be upset and played by a complete stranger only brings more feelings of shame. He has found out the hard way that the whole Gotta-Aid incident was a set-up from the start. *How could I have been so stupid as to believe 'that guy' over Helen, and then pass my anger off on Manohar?*

*

They enter the residential block, stroll through the foyer, and pass the security desk unquestioned. Ali and Mohammed chat in Indonesian and Manohar nods a lot in his new kufi hat, carrying a prayer mat like the others, and wearing Yusef's clothes.

They make their way to the elevator, press the button while exchanging discreet smiles, and Manohar slips away down the hall.

Ali and Mohammed will take an elevator ride to nowhere, return, and meet Yusef at the park.

Manohar taps at the New Zealand door without a break, all the while looking up the hall. His heart is racing. Vincent swings it open only halfway, lurching over with an arm across to block any unwanted visitors. He looks Manohar up and down, his eyes asking, *What are you dressed in?*

Manohar ducks under his arm; he is desperate to get out of the hallway. He feels like a spy in enemy territory and wishes for herbal tea and a quiet place to meditate.

Billy jumps to his feet, and the rest whirl around in their seats to face him. Their eyes then fall upon his sarong, asking themselves the same question Vincent has.

Without a word, Manohar rolls out the prayer mat on the floor to reveal his prize: four fish lie there and a nice sized crab springs to attention, walking about threatening the room with its claws. With a bare foot and lots of experience, Vincent pins the crab down from behind and his body begins to rumble with a deep chuckle. Mikey stands up clapping. "Oh cuz, you did good."

*

Helen sits at the head of a full table like a happy matriarch at a long-awaited family reunion. Everyone is together; it is a festive occasion, and for the first time, Billy is eating a hearty breakfast before a competition. It is as close to a level playing field as they will ever get.

Empty plates and fish bones are lying in front of Billy, and his stomach is full. He places his knife and fork down and rubs his belly. With a big grin, he declares, "Man, I feel good. Compliments to the chef. And especially to the best medic ever, AND fisherman. Thank you, Manohar."

Vincent takes a bow, and the table gives a cheer for Manohar, "I could not have done it without the help of our friends. And now I have such a great story to tell."

Vincent scrapes all the bones together on one plate and stacks the dirty dishes together. He leans in towards the last remnants of the crab on the remaining plate. Mikey grabs a fork and raises it over Vincent's hand like a dagger, threatening to stab him. "Get your crazy fucking eyes off that claw, big man. You boiled his crab in my magic water. What is wrong with you? Where is your concept of sharing?"

"NO, you didn't?!" Rob's jaw drops. But a snigger follows. "Haha, you got magic crabs, Mikey."

"That reminds me, I'd better get the bag ready with some fresh towels and water," Aaron says, getting up from the table. "And maybe turn the shower on for YOU?" He suggests to Manohar as he leaves for the Wongii apartment. Manohar sniffs at his hands and clothing.

"Yeah, no offence, but cats will chase you if you go out," says Billy.

Mikey is busy sucking on the crab claw talking to himself, "Only heathens use fresh water to boil crabs. No class whatsoever."

Rob lights up a joint, draws deeply, and exhales long. The pungent smell of marijuana wafts across the table towards Manohar. He waves the smoke away. "This early? Really?"

"It is better than your cologne, man," jokes Rob. "You smell like the end of a salmon run."

Helen giggles, content to sit back and enjoy this 'family' banter, when suddenly, the door bursts open, and Aaron rushes back in with a scowl on his face, "You're not going to believe this. The bastards nicked our jerseys when they dropped the fruit basket off. Fuckers!"

"What?" Helen jumps up.

"Everything," says Aaron. "Everything with a Wongii logo; shorts, shirts, yours, mine …"

The happy family breakfast ends in a stunned silence. They look at each other in search of a solution, each one waiting for the other to speak, hoping someone would at least come up with some options. None are offered, only more silence.

Allisante slaps the table and gets up from it. "Pfff. It is a jersey!"

She scoffs. "*No problema.* One shirt and my skating sash, and Helen and I can make another. Let's go."

"I can't sew!"

"Oh. But you can cut letters out. Possible *los chicas* are there to help as well. But we have all the materials and machines we need."

"Yes …" murmurs Helen. Her eyes flick from Allisante to Billy, to Manohar and beyond, staring into nothing, imagining and contemplating. It is as if she has fallen into a dream. She hasn't. Her mind is racing; it is back at work. "Yes, yes we do."

"I only have an hour to present myself," declares Billy, in a panic.

"*Soy Cubana, Amor,* trust me. We fix everything."

Helen grabs Allisante by the hand and pulls her to the door. "We have work to do." They scramble through the door and down the hallway.

"Amor?" Aaron raises an eyebrow to Mikey.

"That's all I heard," says Mikey.

"Oh, shut up," huffs Billy.

CHAPTER 18

BEHIND THE STARTERS line, runners stretch out and listen intently to last-minute instructions from coaches and trainers. This end of the field is crowded out with all ninety-five Decathlon contestants starting together in the one event.

Aaron cranes his neck and searches for Helen and Allisante between swipes of his phone while Billy works his hamstring, popping his head up intermittently like a second meerkat. There are only minutes to go, and he is still wearing a New Zealand jersey that Mikey has lent him.

"Billy? Have you seen this?" Asks Aaron. He doesn't wait for an answer as he spies Allisante running to trackside, holding up a brown paper bag.

"*Listo,* Aaron. *Listo,*" she yells. Helen and two Cuban women who have helped out with the jersey are right behind her. He runs to the fence to greet them.

Allisante has red lipstick smudged across her face and there is no time to ask why. He grabs the bag from her and she jumps up and down, clapping her hands. When he opens the bag, the Cubana women burst out laughing. He looks at them, confused, then wary. Fondling through the bag, he raises his eyebrows high and looks to Helen for confirmation.

"You will just have to convince him," she urges.

"Oh, I will. Leave it to me," he assures her. He runs across the track and rushes with the bag to Billy.

Billy looks inside and backs away. He looks over to Helen, but she is insistent, stabbing towards the bag with her pointed finger repeatedly.

"No," Billy declares with a mulish look.

"Put it on." Aaron's voice brooks no argument as he drops the bag. "We don't have time for anything else. I'm your coach."

"Uh, uh."

"C'mon. It's a media storm out there for you, and you won't get another crack at this."

But Billy shakes his head again, backing away. He refuses to entertain the idea. Trainers and coaches are called to leave the field. Aaron thinks he should try a different tactic.

"What's the rule of success? What is Uncle Dale's rule of success? Say it."

"Be nice to yourself and ignore people who can't think outside the box."

"And? Be nice to yourself and ignore people who can't think outside the box, and?"

"And try to be nice to them, because they are in a box."

"They are in a box! Fuck that. And fuck trying to be nice to Mr Weeks anymore! GIVE IT BACK TO HIM, Bill! Has looking like the victim of foul play ever helped you before? Ever? Once?"

Billy starts to pace, watching the runners as they move to the lanes. As shameful as it is, he has to concede it is true. Many times, he has finished second or even dead last according to Jack's skulduggery. All because Jack has a bet going on to take some poor fool's money. It is never any use crying over it.

Billy tears his shirt off and snatches at the bag.

*

Everyone has a tactic in mind for themselves to run their particular race.

They have worked on it for years. Those with a big finish come from behind when others were tiring; they have no need to be in front at the starting line. There is space between those athletes.

At the front, it is shoulder to shoulder with over twenty athletes across the eight lanes. For the pacesetters and front runners, it is imperative to be there, and they stand their ground with each other to hold it.

Vying for a front position, Billy worms his way through the back of the pack. *I deserve to be here!* Runners close ranks and block his path; he cannot go any further.

I have a full belly today, and I want to know how I stack up. He cajoles and pushes his way through, to join them one row behind the starting line. It is a solid, unyielding wall of thick shoulders in front.

And fuck trying to be nice, my coach told me, so I am going to find out! Billy puts his head down and barges his way in, creating an unruly Mexican wave down the line.

Lined up but unwelcome, Billy maintains his ground. Sponsorship logos on competitors are clearly seen from here: pharmaceutical brands, easily recognised from unrelated products found in household medicine cabinets the world over; sports shoes far too expensive for the average wage; and clothing labels you need a second job to pay off. All are splashes of bright colours, eye-catching geometric shapes, and clever wording.

However, Billy's midriff is cut off; a white t-shirt with the Wongii logo has been professionally stitched using Allisante's red sash, and the silk shimmers in the sunlight. It is her bright red lipstick kisses around the logo that are a dead giveaway that it's been homemade. And his allotted number 42, front and back, even sits in a picture frame made from her lips.

Squeezed in between China and the USA, the US runner takes a look at Billy and asks, "Did your mother do that?"

The starter walks to the side of the track. "On your mark …Get set …"

"Urrhh." Billy lets out a loud grunt and stomps a foot forward, breaking the line before the gun is fired. It is as intentional as it is loud.

He only takes a couple of small steps, but he manages to incite the hyped-up US runner alongside to follow suit and break the line with him. And the US runner takes enough big strides so that the walk of shame back to the line-up belongs to him and him alone.

The other athletes groan and shake their heads. The US athlete ignores them, and squares blame directly at Billy with a glare.

*

Back home, the crowd is spilling out of the door from the public bar in Wongii. Jack, Janine, Dale, Laddie, and Mary are sitting at a reserved table in the front. After all the meetings, the artwork, the house painting, festival and donations, it has all come down to this. Excitement and tension are holding everyone together: they are glued to the screen. A big sigh rings through the bar when Billy 'false' starts.

A hippie known as New Moon leans in and out at the back of the room trying to focus on the screen, but he can see two. *Maybe I should not have had that second blue pill with the smiley face. I'll switch to diet coke after this bourbon … alcohol is a poison after all.* He covers one eye with his hand and tries his best.

*

Billy repositions himself behind the starting line and waits for the US athlete to nudge his way back in the lineup. Pestering and prodding begins in the field as, once again, they harass for better positions. From left and right, Billy cops it. The starter takes his place, once again: "On your mark … Get—"

Billy jumps out and runs ten metres before slowing down to a stop at fifteen.

"Aarrgh!" He hears someone cry in frustration from behind. *Stop being nice. Stop being nice,* he reminds himself.

TIM: *A second false start. Nerves are showing today, Kym.*

KYM: *Yes, last chance for Billy Uke before disqualification.*

*

The entire bar lets out an exhaustive loud sigh, and those who can't take the pressure have to turn away. But this time, worried talk follows. New Moon tries to keep up with the conversations but gazes about the room, dazed instead. Jack cocks an eye. "That's not nerves. That's Aaron," he declares.

"Yep. My boy doesn't start anything early. Especially that early," Laddie agrees.

Mary and Janine, and anyone else that has heard him, look at Jack, wondering what he is talking about. He motions them back to the screen: Billy is dawdling like he has no place to go, as he makes his way back to the starting line.

"What is he doing?" Janine asks.

"Advertising. He's advertising," chuckles Dale.

*

The starter begins once more: "On your mark …" Billy sinks low into his stance.

"Get set …"

Billy sinks lower. He pushes a leg through the runners behind, forcing them to make room.

BANG!

Billy bolts out and streaks away like his mother's life depends on it. It is a twenty-five-metre dash, or all hope is lost. He pulls away from the field from the get-go. The remaining athletes stick to game plans and previously discussed tactics, all starting conservatively for a five-kilometre Cross Country.

Far in the lead, after only twenty metres, there is no slowing, only a skip in his step as Billy throws a hand behind his head. Reaching inside his shirt, he unfurls a red silk cape sewn into the neckline. Billy pounds the pavement, sprinting further and further ahead. His red cape flutters behind, a large white 'W' in the middle. It has been sewn from the bottom end of his cut off t-shirt, to show where he is from.

Officials in the middle of the stadium, who are in the process of placing flags or measuring lines for future events, stop and gawk. Trainers and coaches stop talking and take their eyes off their own charges to stare at Billy. Throughout the stadium, movement ceases like there is a funeral procession passing. It is a complete stupefied silence.

Allisanta's voice rings out, "*Tengo un hero. Tengo un hero.*" [I have a hero.] The Cuban ladies wail with laughter and slip into celebratory salsa steps.

Vincent's eyes widen, and Mikey places a hand on his shoulder. "Man, I told you my water had magic powers." Vincent chuckles hard.

Helen looks up to Mr Week's office.

*

In the Wongii Hotel, a stillness falls. An unheard of quiet is in the place, before Dale bangs the table and he and Jack roar with laughter.

People spit out their drinks, unable to contain their amusement. The place erupts and the carpet soaks up gallons of beer.

Janine and Mary sit still watching, mesmerised, with their hands over their mouths. New Moon thinks someone has changed the channel.

*

TIM: *What is he doing?*

KYM: *Yes, absolute madness to set off like that Tim. This is five kilometres, not a 100-metre sprint.*

TIM: *I am speaking of the cape, Kym.*

KYM: *Oh, I like it!*

Stunned into immobility, Mr Weeks cannot fathom what he is seeing. Or process what he should do. He is frozen at his office window, gawking at a dark-skinned Superman screaming ahead of the Titan drug-filled pack. A hero's cape is mocking their sponsorship for all the world to see.

Mr Weeks' body twists with an urge to act, and act fast, but his feet stay planted, not knowing where to go. He cannot pull his head away from what is unfolding before him. Control has been lost. It is too late. There is nothing to be done.

*

The 100-metre mark is just ahead, and Billy is still running at full clip.

The stadium exit is halfway around the track's bend, another fifty metres. He backs off just a touch, nevertheless maintaining a pace that is faster than his opponents, and eases somewhat into the turn.

Billy reaches the stadium tunnel to exit and comes to a dead stop. Hands on hips, he draws deep breaths, pokes his chest out like a DC comic character, and turns around to face the other runners. He waits and soaks up more camera time. He only gets a few breaths, mere seconds really, but it is enough to get tongues wagging; it will put him on the cover of magazines.

TIM: *Unsure about the sportsmanship here, Kym. This is not what sport is about.*

KYM: *Pfff. It is YouTube gold, and a thousand memes right there. This is exactly what it's about, Tim.*

As the pack reached him, they jostle for the tunnel. Billy needs another breath first. Stoic faces refuse to look at him, concentrating on their game plan. But when he makes out the face of the US runner, the athlete gifts him with a smile. He is unsure if it is a smile of pity and wonder at the foolishness, or admiration at the sheer brazen behaviour, but it is not anger. He takes it as an omen and rejoins the field, resuming midway in the pack, to enter the tunnel.

In the darker privacy of the tunnel, while they are packed together, a hand grabs at Billy's cape. It yanks him off balance, tearing the stitches from his shirt, and it sends him crashing out the exit to the ground.

TIM: *Oh, and there has been a fall!*

No sooner does Billy hit the tarmac than a Lebanese runner scoops a hand under his armpit. The Scottish runner scoops under the other growling, "Get up, Laddie!" Between the two, they haul him to his feet.

KYM: *Now there is some sportsmanship for you, Tim.*

Five strides later, Billy tears his cape off and throws it aside. Play time is over. Aaron has got what he wanted, and it is his time now.

Billy settles in with the runners and keeps up the pace. He has no game plan, and he is unconcerned with such matters. What matters now is his breathing and running his own race, regardless of what others are doing.

The course involves another 200-metres on the road surface before stepping onto the grass. A number of small obstacle barriers only 45 centimetres high lie spread out across the grass. Not high enough to bother anybody—as they are all trained for hurdles after all—but enough to force runners to change their step.

The track then winds its way down closer to the beach and the pack is still tightly knitted jumping the barriers, except for a dozen front runners that intend to lead all the way.

Billy loves running on grass. It is what he is most accustomed to. He and Aaron have had daily runs beginning at the Buckman's back door and across eighty acres just to get started. He clears the obstacles with ease and finds his rhythm. They are one kilometre into the race and Billy lets his natural stride dictate the pace. He knows that he will still have a little in reserve that way.

The shorter, stocky athletes who performed well in shot put will not give in and they keep their pace, never expecting to get a place. Their times will just count towards the final points tally. However, the length of a runner's stride comes into play, and those with it stretch out across the turfed field.

Billy makes sure each breath is deep. Shallow breathing is too much work and will not supply the oxygen needed. *Concentrate!* He reminds himself.

Some athletes start to make their move and take advantage of this section. Billy is not going to let them get away. He steps out from the pack with them. It is another 600-metres on good, level grass to the beach and he stays with them all the way.

TIM: *Approaching two kilometres in, and the field starts to stretch. But Billy Uke has not dropped off as expected. Surely, he has eaten this morning, Kym?*

KYM: *I don't think that is any longer the issue. The issue is being well placed amongst the chemically enhanced athletes, Tim. That is his whole point, I believe.*

*

The large screens provided at various intervals behind the fence line to the track are surrounded by scores of onlookers; from here they can watch the happenings of the Decathlon taking place outside of the stadium.

Helen, Manohar, Aaron, and Allisante are joined by the New Zealanders and the two Cuban women. They encourage their contestants from afar and wait for them to return to the stadium. All are staring up at a screen.

"Run Billy! Stay with them. Stay up there," Aaron urges.

"Go. Go," adds Manohar.

Vincent looks away from the screen and down to the middle of the field. Security guards arrive and begin talking to the officials. He peruses the track and fence line to see more guards at the finishing line talking into their collars. He doesn't like the look of that. Not after the drama of the yucca incident. He recalls how they'd taken Billy's food. And they had harassed his newfound friends. He sets off for the nearest track entrance to the finishing line, brushing past Mikey as he leaves.

"Oh, ho! Ahh, Rob? The big man is on the move," declares Mikey.

Rob looked to Vincent, then to where he was headed, "Ooh shit." He takes off after him.

Mikey follows. Helen sees Aaron turn his head, and soon the whole troupe is in hot pursuit to prevent any trouble.

"Mind you. This could be epic to watch, cuz!" Declares Mikey.

"No, Mikey, no." Rob shakes his head.

*

At the two-kilometre mark, the course turns to run along a strip. It is not far back from the beach and goes for another kilometre before turning back towards the stadium. The manicured grass fields finish, and the grass here is thinner and grows on a sandier base. It is much softer. Soft enough to see the footprints and divots left from the front runners. It is a killer on the calf muscles.

Billy sets himself a task of keeping the same pace along this stretch and lets attrition take its toll on the competitors' legs.

The group begins to close the distance on the front runners. It may be truer to say that the front runners cease to pull away, and a few of them drop back from the front. Billy's calves can feel the difference. But the pack he is in hold their positions for a long time, and the halfway point is flagged very well up just ahead. Billy has no doubt that all the athletes have plans and moves to make as they come into the final stretch of the race.

The moment he passes the marker, six runners step out from behind, and three ahead of him challenge their leader. He remains in his step, no quicker no slower, his breathing is meditative.

TIM: *Lack of drugs starting to show over the distance as Billy Uke drops from 18th to 24th.*

More hurdles mark the 2.8-and 2.9-kilometre intervals and the manicured grass begins again at the three-kilometre mark.

Billy holds his pace, heading into the first hurdle, and grinds back three places before the long-legged Kenyan passes him on the next. By the time he has changed over onto the grass proper, Billy has picked up two more places, but another has already passed him. The athletes whose tactics are to come from behind are starting to position themselves, ready to make their final burst.

This has nothing to do with him. He knows that is a battle that will be fought in the distance, in the last hundred metres, probably. Front runners vs back. Lots of runners won't even see it. Better he concerns himself with himself, and the competition that is about him. The sand has been gruelling; it has worn some athletes down, but Billy is now back to good grass, and he is glad to be. He starts to stalk closer to the two guys ahead.

Trinidad comes from behind, runs along with him for fifty metres, and then passes the two guys ahead. This athlete is known to snatch the lead from behind in a sustained final burst of speed. He is a danger to both the front runners and the Kenyan. He overtakes Billy, who is measuring his own breath and speed. He lets him get a few steps ahead and decides this athlete is as good a measuring stick as any; he will track this guy. He doesn't have to keep up all the way, but he will see how long he can go. He has estimated there is still 1.7 kilometres left to run.

Weaving around pairs and pushing by a group of three, Billy stays on the Trinidadian like he is momma bear on her cub. They move to the front of the second pack, and he can see the Kenyan is not far ahead. He fights hard to regulate his breathing, and although his legs and chest are not burning yet, he can feel the heat gathering. There is a little over one kilometre to go when Trinidad starts to pull away from him, but Billy has caught up to his first front runner. The stadium is just ahead.

He will maintain this speed a little longer and not chase him. He is closing in on two more, anyway. Soon the grass will end, and the final 600-metre road stretch will begin: 250-metres around the stadium, and a 350-metre lap inside to the finishing line. He will have to wait until then for any final burst that he has. Billy passes the pair; one is the US athlete.

There is fifty metres of grass left, when something clicks, and he starts to throw everything he has into it. *I have to know!* Falling victim to impatience, he cannot wait any longer. He strides out as fast as he can manage. His legs have fuel today and they are burning hot with it now. His stomach is still fairly full and quiet, but his chest is starting to scream out.

Billy pushes and pushes again. He picks up another place and thinks that maybe there are fifteen athletes ahead. But the leaders are already turning into the stadium.

The runner from the US reappears to his right. He plunges along for a moment until his superior strength began to show. He manages to produce a sustained power run and turns into the tunnel, ten steps ahead of Billy. He is next passed by the Moroccan in the tunnel, and on exiting for the inner track, the Kenyan, Trinidad, and Algeria are fighting it out going into the final turn to the home straight.

Billy gives it all that he has, but he is already asking his body for as much as it can give. Void of scientific compounds and 'magical' drugs, he is solely powered by a fish and crab. There isn't any faster anymore, there is just hold out for as long as you can.

TIM: *Billy Uke doggedly tries to hold on to 17th spot.*

KYM: *Whatever bone he is chewing on, keep chewing, Tim. Outstanding effort.*

*

The press is hanging over the fence line, brawling for positions at the entrances to the track. They wait for the finish line to be crossed so they can break the line. Security guards stand before them to ensure they don't break early. The Wongii Troupe is standing behind the media, and Manohar is wasting soothing words on Vincent.

*

By the end of the first straight, Billy is beginning to advance on the exhausted Spaniard who has tried to front run the whole way. But others are gaining on him. Billy can hear the roar of the entourages cheering the battle taking place up front in the last straight. Through sheer determination, he overtakes the Spaniard on the turn.

His chest is searing hot, and his legs are aflame. *Push it. Push it now and you will find out! Just 150-metres to know.* The field is closing in on him. Runners that are behind start to bustle and move wide. Billy can see them out of the corner of his eye. Up ahead, the Kenyan crosses the finish line two steps in front of Trinidad.

Three runners battled it out wider, but he has the inside lead coming into the straight. *More. I need a little more.* With every fibre of discipline, every thread of hope and aspiration, he forces his will upon his body.

They continue to creep up on him like a dark shadow … a shadow that grows larger as more join in. With seventy metres to go, they catch him, and it is four wide, running down the straight. More runners lurk behind them, trying to find a way through or around. *More. I need more.*

But his legs stretch no further in their stride; there is no increase in their speed, and a runner overtakes him. Billy's body is maxed out and can give no more. With thirty-five metres left, another passes. He is now only one of seven athletes spread across the lanes; seven athletes competing over thirty-five metres.

It is the most important thirty-five metres of his life, and only thirty-five metres at that, but it is gruelling on the body and mind. It is him and him alone. There is no more to give, but he will give them nothing. Nothing left, but he will not let them take his nothing. They cross the finish in a tight line. He is certain that one has pipped him just before, though. He just cannot hold out any longer.

He doesn't look up to the placings scoreboard to see that he has finished twentieth; he is too busy looking at his shoes and heaving for oxygen. He knows that it was the best he could do. That it has used all of him. And he has succeeded in killing the 'if'. Theory is dead. Any laurels or shortcomings are owned. He now knows how he has sized up with performance-enhanced athletes, for better or worse, over the five-kilometre cross country.

CHAPTER 19

THE PRESS IS in a frenzy. They lack a focal point, yet just have to be 'first'. First. Live. But there are two stories from the same moment in time. They buzz like sickly bees torn between two queens. First is what counts. First is a story in itself, and he is Kenyan and catching his breath, ready to go.

First to the story is different. It depends on what the story is. What matters the most? First place or twentieth? The camera operators want to know more than anyone. They are sick of stop-starts, changes of mind, and tripping over each other. All they want is for their charges to make up their fucking minds!

Questions rage at the Kenyan, for a moment, but he takes too long answering. He is still struggling for breath between a dozen journalists' questions. *The Koori Australian won't be any better*, some journalists start to think. *But if he has trouble answering, it may be MY question he struggles with ... As long as I'm there FIRST!* Journalists start to abandon the winner in a race of their own. Billy has now crossed the line and is vulnerable.

Jill the photojournalist is there first. "Did you eat today?"

"What does the red cape symbolise?" Interjects Channel 4.

"Why was your cape red? Are you a communist?" Lachlan News wants to know.

Gasping for air, Billy is in no state to answer questions yet. Four security guards come together, and with outstretched arms, they herd the press back a few steps. Track officials stand to the side out of their way. More athletes cross the line.

"Have you eaten?" Channel 3 calls past security.

"Okay. Okay! You can all ask your questions as soon as the officials have finished their business," a guard cries out.

An official steps forward and in a loud public speaking voice, announces, "Billy Uke! You shall present yourself for a urine sample immediately."

*

Vincent strides across the track lanes with the Wongii Troupe: the New Zealanders follow closely behind. The crowd is building past the finish line and more guards arrive. But he is almost there.

"Urine sample? You have to do something," Aaron tells Helen.

"They have the right to ask. There is nothing I can do."

"They cannot be trusted," declares Manohar.

"No. They can't." She stops walking. She pulls her phone out and starts fiddling with it.

Billy is just there and yet she goes no further. Manohar, Aaron, and Allisante hesitate. *Why has she stopped?* The Wongii Team look at each other, puzzled. *Is that what she was doing last night on her phone? Was she talking to Weeks?* The thought runs through Aaron's mind.

"If a sample is not supplied to us, you will be disqualified from the Games," the official continues.

"Helen!" Aaron yells in despair.

"The race is over. It's how the results are spun now," Helen states.

"What is that supposed to mean?"

"Let me do my job, Aaron. Go do yours," Helen snaps.

TIM: *And I am being told there are questions being asked of young Billy Uke. Officials require a sample for analysis, Kym.*

KYM: *Oh, please. I question where you find a sterile environment to test anything in Guantanamo. Do we even have drug testing facilities?*

Vincent heads straight towards Billy and the guard that is standing over him. Two new security guards arrive in an effort to cut the New Zealanders off, but he makes a hard right turn and walks directly into them. They don't quite know what to do with a man like Vincent, who towers over them. He blocks them long enough for Mikey and Rob, and the Wongii Troupe to get to Billy and surround him.

This is something new the press has not seen before. It reactivates the furore. Camera operators and photographers vie for better positions. It is a standoff on a racetrack.

"What's she doing?" Billy asks Aaron.

"Helen says the race is over."

Billy's heart sinks. He thinks of the job offer. He looks at Helen, but she doesn't make eye contact; she is too busy with her phone.

"Stand aside," Mr Daniels, the Security Chief instructs them.

The Wongii Troupe pulls the circle closer. There is no way they are going to let Billy be led away by security. "Move away!" He raises his voice above the buzz.

The flash of cameras is constant now. A journalist skirts security and steps out from the media crowd. She walks wide, around the flanks, and makes sure she is seen by her press colleagues.

Purposefully, she steps into the fray, waving papers above her head and a man in a suit follows her. "Excuse me. Excuse me, I'm Alicia Jade from the Evening Post, and this is our lawyer. We have a contract with—"

"That's all well and good, but your interview will have to wait until after his urine sample is given," the Security Chief barks. "Now please move back!"

"Given? No, no, no. We paid $100,000 for whatever is in his

bladder. This is a contract of ownership of Mr Uke's urine, not for an interview." The newspaperwoman hands him the document and points to Helen, who is livestreaming him. "A bill of sale, if you prefer. Testing will be independent and shared live to all news services. But that urine belongs to us!" She states.

Mr Daniels flinches and gives a quick inspection to the first page of the documents. And while he flinches, the lawyer distributes copies to officials and other journalists. "Well … we are under no obligation to grant you access to our facilities," Mr Daniels advises Alicia.

"Then, man, you better take a whizz right here," Mikey says.

"What?!" Billy pants in distress. "No."

"Yeah, yeah, right," Aaron agrees.

Alicia is fully prepared and passes a specimen bottle to Aaron. Aaron passes it back to Billy. Billy holds it in dismay. Disbelief too … He shoots a look at Helen; she is filming him.

Not to be outdone, the Chief calls up the Titan Doctor he has standing by. The doctor bends down and opens his medical bag. Mr Danials steps in closer between Vincent and Mikey. "But we have a right to his blood."

To the surprise of all, Vincent complies immediately and steps out of Mr Daniel's way. His second step, however, is directly onto the doctor's bag. His foot lands to the crunch of broken glass, and he gives a silent, open-handed apology to the doctor; it is shown as an act of innocence in an unfortunate accident. Helen is loving the live streaming of these shenanigans to the world.

"What do you think you're doing over there?" Mikey shrieks. "Get back in the line-up, big man."

With a newfound vigour, Vincent bounds onto the bag again in his return … with reclaimed pride. He has given up on the idea of ever being in a line-up or a scrum again. It has been six years since his banishment from rugby. He smiles in Mr Daniel's face. "Hee, hee. He said line-up."

The Chief is livid and cannot hide it: his face glows red, and his fists clenched, while in Cape Town, a South African named Fred, bangs on a table roaring with laughter. Fred's friends cheer and whoop along at Vincent's antics.

The Chief motions for more guards to join him, and for officials to move back. For a moment, Aaron thinks they are going to be stormed, and he braces himself, but the guards are headed off by three strangers who join the circle. Mohamed, Yusef, and Ali stand in front of Manohar and Aaron, and they all lock arms.

The press snaps away at the potential confrontation. The world is watching.

*

Billy's eyes tear up. He is trying his best, but everybody is watching. Waiting. *They are filming for god's sake!* His mind screams at him. He strains and strains.

"No pressure, but I'll bet 200 million people are waiting for you to piss," Aaron reminds him, barely suppressing a smirk.

"I'm trying."

"Drink. Flush yourself." Manohar passes a water bottle from behind. Billy chugs on it.

"Think of a waterfall," Rob suggests. "And stop pressuring him. Everybody be quiet."

"Being heard doesn't help!" Billy shoots back.

Head down in his endeavour, both hands full, he shuffles around in a spin, away from the media, as much as possible. Billy cannot turn his back on everyone, though, as he is out in the open. *But at least some of the press!* It is worth a go.

Billy makes sure the bottle is lined up and glances up to see how he has done and what privacy he has accomplished. And there is the US runner he tricked at the starting line. His legs are apart, arms folded, and he looks like his very own Superman on happy gas.

His toothy smile beams amongst the mayhem and pressure, and forces Billy to smile as well. It is only fair; it is payback. And when the man throws his head back, relishing the moment, and laughs out loud at Billy's obvious embarrassment, Billy cannot help but laugh back. It still doesn't help though; not really. He still has his penis out, an empty bottle, and no doubt his mother is watching. He wants this over with.

*

Helen relaxes and holds back a smile. It is quite the spectacle: eight people from four countries, with their backs to Billy, arms locked in a protective circle. But there should be nine. Oh! Allisante is facing the wrong way.

Standing on her tippy toes, oblivious to the pressure, she is peeking over Rob's shoulder, doing her best to see Billy's penis. She looks back at Helen with wide eyes. Tilting her head, she beckons for Helen to come see. "Look!" she calls.

Helen immediately lets go of the phone with her left hand, doing her best to keep it steady with her right. She leans out from behind it and drops her hand wide. With a raised eyebrow, she silently implores, *How on earth is that appropriate?*

"You're not helping, Ally," Aaron tells her.

Allisante bounds away from the circle and skips over to Helen. "You are so clever. You knew."

"Men like Weeks are predictable, Ally."

Meanwhile, a tear runs down Billy's cheek.

"Mate. It's the EASIEST job in the world," Aaron prompts over his shoulder.

"I'm trying."

"Wish someone would pay me to stand around urinating," Rob pines.

"Guys? I really, really need to take a piss," says Mikey.

"Ah, for Christ's sake, Mikey, just hold on to it," Rob scolds.

"For fuck's sake! Do you know how unhealthy that is? I'm an athlete."

Vincent rolls his eyes and drops his head in scepticism.

"It's a hundred grand for urinating, is what I'm saying. I could do it," Rob theorises. "Maybe for less?"

"Ooh, is that a tinkle?" Manohar beams a smile. "I think it is. I think we have a tinkle, ladies and gentlemen." He raises his voice, "We have tinkle!"

The press laps it up. Laughter sweeps through the crowd and the flash of cameras is like a strobe light. People begin to clap and cheer while Billy urinates.

*

In a darkened room with curtains drawn, the Media Mogul sits forward in his lounge. He pours himself a morning scotch. It is not something that he usually does, but what is unfolding in the arena is genuinely of interest to him. Multiple screens from networks he owns display the standoff, the tension, and the conflict. There are tears on Billy's face, and furthermore, there is a show of sporting comradery. Hell, there is even a lawyer on the track like a courtroom drama.

"I think we have tinkle!" At this announcement, different angles of Billy peeing appear on his screens. They show close-ups and Billy's strained facial expressions. People are clapping. One screen flicks over to Helen, who is livestreaming.

Drink in hand, the Media Mogul stands and tips it to her. He begins to chuckle; it is a low rumble in his belly. "Oh, well played. Well played. Now THAT is a story!"

*

The lawyer removes his coat and hands it to Alicia Jade. He stands before the press, puts on a pair of gloves, and shows both sides of his hands to them, before reaching into Billy's circle of people with one hand. He steps back out from the group and holds up the urine sample for all to see. Billy covers his face in embarrassment.

Waving about a test strip in his other hand, like a magician would in a show—nothing up my sleeve— the lawyer dips the strip into the bottled sample and puts the sample bottle down. He then displays a colour chart, before lying it down on the track before the media and placing them together.

People push closer to see. The wait is intense. They all want to be the first to report. Everything goes quiet. The silence is agitating and deafening.

The lawyer's eyes flick from the chart to the crowd, and back, as people lean in. Mikey is doing a little jig, needing the bathroom. Vincent steadies him with a hand on his shoulder.

From the Wongii Hotel to South Africa, people are glued to the screen. The quad bikers and slingshot crew are gathered on a porch fixated on an old television.

The lawyer stands up with a grin and displays the result to the cameras. "Clear!" He announces loudly and strides the line, making sure everyone can compare the colours.

The crowd erupts with cheers and applause. Mikey bolts through them for the toilet. The circle breaks and Allisante rushes to Billy. The press follows.

Helen, though, walks away. This is Billy's moment. *Let him enjoy it,* she sighs with relief and joy. She leaves the track and celebrations and wanders out to the middle of the stadium. Momentarily, she stops and, triumphantly, she looks up to Mr Weeks' office: she knows he is there watching.

*

Mr Weeks watches on; a tremble begins on his bottom lip. He glares at Helen, standing out on the field alone. It is like she has set fire to the fire station, and it is spreading. *This is my field! My games! But now there will be a reckoning,* he ponders ominously. This has happened on his watch, at his games. He was supposed to manage problems, not let them escalate.

Helen holds her phone above her head and his phone beeps. He draws it out of his pocket and checks it. It is a message from Helen. *THERE IS NO HONEY. You bastards are killing the bees.*

He stands back, and filled with rage, he lines up Helen. He throws his phone at her as hard as he can. It smashes against the glass and bounces across the room. Helen can only imagine his reaction but walks away, content. There is a delighted spring in her step.

Mr Weeks is left trembling. He reaches for his pills.

CHAPTER 20

BILLY UKE CLEARED IN PUBLIC URINATION is the first headline to hit the press. Aaron loves it.

WONGII TITAN HAS CLEAN URINE comes next.

Lachlan News runs a headline stating, *COMMUNISTS PEE IN PUBLIC*, along with a picture of the red cape.

SUPERHERO PEE WORTH $100,000 is Helen's favourite.

The party continues on the streets of Cape Town. The Koori kids have fallen asleep by firelight after ad lib rap songs of Billy have been shared to the sound of the didgeridoo. Everyone has had a go.

The Cuban pueblo is alive with music and success. They have pooled their money and bought beer: they feel rich. Rich with a sense of achievement. They toast The Man Who Cut the Wire as they dance, and he sleeps. Jose snores on, with four empty beer bottles in front of him this time. While in an undisclosed location, the two camo-clothed American bloggers question the results.

In the Wongii Hotel, it is very late and there is mayhem. People are plastered. Even the bartender is drunk and passing out the wrong drinks. Nobody cares.

Forty-year-old drunk men who have never tried marijuana decide it is a good time to try. It isn't. They follow the hippies outside, have two totes on a joint, and immediately green-out. They are left to sleep it off in the beer garden. Their wives shake their heads: *Stupid!*

*

It has been hours since the Decathlon finished, and the New Zealand apartment is turning into a party. Mohammed and friends are there, a salsa song is playing, and the jovial Cuban women are teaching anyone who is interested how to dance to it. Rob has acquired beer from the canteen.

"No eating until we get to Annotto Bay," Aaron has warned Billy, while holding a chicken leg the size of his fist.

Helen has agreed. "We are out of here first thing in the morning. You will just have to hold out till then. We have to maintain our credibility, I'm afraid."

Vincent comes down the stairs carrying the last remaining six-pack of Mikey's water. Mikey runs to him, hamming it up, and throws his arms around him while he is still on the second step. His head rests on Vincent's belly, and laughter fills the room at the sight.

"Yes. I love you big man, I love you."

"So, see you next games, Helen?" Rob mocks her with a wry grin.

"Ha, no chance." Helen laughs, "But I'm sure you'll see Billy around. We are getting so many sponsorship offers."

"Oh, and Helen? No more red capes. Ever!" Billy declares.

"My superhero," Allisante snuggles in.

"Captain Eggplant," Manohar retorts with a grin.

"... And the Piss Kid!" Rob continues.

Aaron and Yusef exchange glances, and Yusef reaches for a bag. "Well, Yusef has a surprise for us."

He opens the bag and produces the red cape. Yusef receives a round of applause and back pats, to calls of, "You are a genius," and for Billy to "put it on."

"And I talked to mum," Aaron interjects. "She said a sports collector has offered Wongii fifty grand for this."

"But we never take the first offer, Captain Eggplant," announces Helen. "I'll get a bidding war happening."

Billy shakes his head at being called 'Captain Eggplant'.

"That sounds like you are sticking around," says Manohar.

CHAPTER 21

SINCE THE NEWS broke of Billy, tourism in Wongii has picked up immeasurably; the workers at the local cafe are run off their feet. The town hall no longer sits empty between meetings but is used as an art gallery with all works for sale. Accommodation is full, as is the bar, and the new visitors all leave with local organic produce. Fire twirling through the town is a nightly event that enthrals the children. They have decided to leave Laddie's deck and the giant ring toss intact as a free game for visiting families.

More alternative people and hippies arrive from around the state and stay the weekend to the sound of electronic trance music beating out from the buses with no wheels. Bonfires blaze through the night so that latecomers can find their way around this regional town.

'Discus Golf' is now played to a much larger crowd, and visitors have a try. Vans full of rugby players challenge each other. Insurance waivers are signed and helmets are provided for twenty dollars. And Jack doesn't care if they are sober or not. "An idiot is an idiot," is all he says.

At the Buckman farm, a casual get-together is organised for the committee and artists that have devoted so much of their time. Mary and Laddie Uke along with the extended family and children, Dale,

Julian, little Emmy and her mum, and Mr Exley, are all present. Tables are butted together, set out on the lawn, and filled with nibbles and salads. Mary hugs Manohar, as Janine places more food out and calls to the children playing with Rubi.

"Okay kids. Come get something to eat," Janine urges.

"I have some news," Helen tells the gathering. "Billy, I received an official invitation from Cuba today for us to go visit their organic farms. 'All you can eat', it says. Ha! It will give you an opportunity to visit Allisante."

Billy's face lights up. He is already missing her, even though they have been video chatting every second day.

"My boy still needs a manager," Laddie states, scratching at his head. "I'm getting calls at home from roll-on deodorant companies. Do you know how it feels to have a deodorant company call you? It's like a nasty intervention!"

"And I don't trust anyone else," states Billy.

Helen becomes a little emotional. After everything that has happened, she has earned his trust.

"See, I told you all you had to do was put a t-shirt on him," Jack tells her.

Helen and Manohar exchange dubious glances. "Ha!" Retorts Manohar. "If you only knew."

"And the Wongii Development Fund has suddenly found itself in the position of having enough funds and investors ... but no Project Manager," Janine interjects. "So, the committee voted last night to give you first offer."

"Project Manager?" It is a prize that Helen has not considered. It is the job she needs. Touched that the town, and her new friends, have so much confidence in her, she has to reach for a tissue.

Dale leaves Jack's side and goes to her. He puts his arm around her. "Say yes, and you can have Rubi's first kid. I dressed her up as Gandalf at the fundraiser and slipped her in with the other nannies after Jack left." He smiles at Jack, "Turns out your Sir Linneus likes a bit of wizardry."

"You what?" Jack barks.

Mr Exley, Laddie and Mary roar with laughter at Jack. His face drops, and so does Rubi. The children running alongside her on their way to the table, stop in their tracks.

Four-and five-year-old children stand aghast around Rubi who is lying there with her legs up. She isn't moving. Worried faces look to each other for help. A tear runs down one's cheek, "Rubi?"

EPILOGUE

HELEN STANDS BEFORE an old house, with an unkempt garden. The Uke family and Buckman family are by her side. They wait, brushes in hand, for her to apply the first stroke of orange paint. As she steps forward and starts, they all joined in.

A group of hippies and alternatives, led by Dale and Rubi, march across the paddock to her new home to help out. They carry rakes and shovels, but Dale carries Rubi's first-born kid— Tottering Tom, or TT, as Helen has named him.

THE END

Printed in Dunstable, United Kingdom